D0904182

Barrie Roberts was born in Hampshire in 1939 and educated at Churcher's College, Petersfield. He has been an art student, civil servant, cable technician, music shop manager, folk singer, freelance journalist, printer, computer programmer, further education lecturer and manager of a large student's union.

For most of the last thirty years he has been a criminal lawyer, working for two firms in the West Midlands including work on the appeals of the Birmingham Six.

He is the author of three previous Chris Tyroll mysteries and five Sherlock Holmes books.

His hobbies consist of lazing about and reading about crimes and unsolved mysteries and occasionally going out to buy more books.

BAD PENNY BLUES

When Aussie social historian Sheila McKenna is in the UK, she buys an old penny — one that has been used as a farewell token by a Victorian convict about to be transported. Starting from the inscription on the coin, she sets out to track down the convict's family. With the help of her lawyer fiancé, Chris Tyroll, Sheila narrows the search down to six possible families. They all have stories to tell — of illegitimacy, desertion, and even murder — and they are only too happy to tell them. But unpleasant things have started to happen and slowly the couple realise that someone is trying to stop them . . .

Books by Barrie Roberts
Published by The House of Ulverscroft:

SHERLOCK HOLMES AND
THE MAN FROM HELL
ROBBERY WITH MALICE

BARRIE ROBERTS

BAD PENNY BLUES

Complete and Unabridged

ULVERSCROFT
Leicester

First published in Great Britain in 2000 by
Constable & Robinson Ltd
London

First Large Print Edition
published 2002
by arrangement with
Constable & Robinson Ltd
London

British Library CIP Data

Roberts, Barrie, *1939 –*
    Bad penny blues.—Large print ed.—
    Ulverscroft large print series: mystery
    1. Tyroll, Chris (Fictitious character)—Fiction
    2. Lawyers—Great Britain—Fiction
    3. Detective and mystery stories
    4. Large type books
    I. Title
    823.9′14 [F]

    ISBN 0–7089–4685–2

Published by
F. A. Thorpe (Publishing) Ltd.
Anstey, Leicestershire

Set by Words & Graphics Ltd.
Anstey, Leicestershire
Printed and bound in Great Britain by
T. J. International Ltd., Padstow, Cornwall

This book is printed on acid-free paper

Author's Note

The Metropolitan Borough of Belston does not exist. If it did, it would probably be one of the so-called 'Black Country Boroughs' that lie north-west of Birmingham; since it doesn't, it isn't! All characters, events and organisations in this story are completely fictitious.

Tokens like the penny in the story did, however, exist. Some of them have survived to this day and are much sought after by people who understand what they are and the tragic histories they commemorate.

Web-surfers may be interested to know that the website addresses quoted were genuine at the time of writing.

1

Sheila switched on the light before I could stop her. As I reached her, I heard her choked gasp of dismay, then she turned quickly towards me, burying her face in my shoulder, panting and cursing under her breath. Behind her I could see the pool of bright, fresh blood glistening on the pale stone.

I never imagined it would come to blood on my own doorstep. It had seemed a good idea, one that couldn't do anyone harm — except maybe to their pride. I imagined it as just a sort of historical jigsaw puzzle if I imagined at all. From the beginning I sometimes tried to imagine the people who had been involved.

★   ★   ★

Sawney was sitting the other side of my desk, banging away about his suspended sentence. It was late in the afternoon after a night's celebration and I wasn't in the mood for any ungrateful client, let alone Julian Nugent Sawney. He was the youngest son of a decent family in Warwickshire and had been set adrift in his teens when his father finally faced the fact that his offspring was a compulsive thief. I could forgive that — after all, if there were no repetitive criminals lawyers would be pushed to make a living. What I couldn't forgive was that he was one of my clients and a nasty little git. Apart from thieving, he had three other bad habits — endless moaning that it was somebody else's fault, dyeing his thinning hair ludicrous colours, and living.

I had got him off a number of petty dishonesty charges (and nothing was too small for him to steal) and I reckoned he had been lucky to catch a suspended sentence last time around. I also shared the court's vain hope that a suspended sentence would make him stop and think, in which case I might never see him again. Apparently we were both wrong.

'The trouble is, Mr Tyroll,' he whined, 'if I am accused of anything else while the sentence is suspended, I'll have to serve the sentence.'

'No,' I said. 'If you're convicted of something else while the sentence is suspended you'll have to serve the suspended sentence and a sentence for the new offence. That's the way it's supposed to work. If you don't commit any other crimes, the suspended sentence won't operate.'

'But that's the whole point,' he exclaimed. 'I have been accused of something new!'

'You didn't do it, of course,' I said, deadpan.

'No, of course not,' he said.

'Tell me about it,' I said wearily.

'I live in a boarding house,' he said. 'One of the other lodgers had a very expensive portable radio and it went missing. He called the police and they found the radio in another lodger's room.'

'Not yours?' I interjected.

'Certainly not!' he said, huffily. 'It was a girl on the ground floor.'

'I don't see what this has got to do with you.'

'She said I asked her to steal it, Mr Tyroll. Can you imagine that? She told the police that we had a relationship and that I asked her to steal Mr Thomas's radio. Now they've questioned me about it.'

'And what have you said?'

'Me? That I don't know anything about it, of course.'

'Did you have a relationship with this girl?'

'Good Lord, no! Well — I asked her out once or twice.'

'Did she go?'

'Well, no.'

'Then, Mr Sawney, you have nothing to worry about. They cannot convict you on the unsupported evidence of an accomplice.'

'But I'm not her accomplice!'

'But you would be if she had told the truth, wouldn't you? As things stand, I doubt if they'll charge you. There's no point — they've got an admission from her that she stole it, why mess about with a dodgy charge against you?'

If I thought I'd wrapped the thing up, I was wrong. He went into a long tirade about how the police had harassed him since his teens, how he was always being wrongly arrested and so on. I let him babble on while my mind drifted . . . to a Dorset beach in the early morning.

It was bitterly cold on the beach, where she had slept all night because an inn was too expensive and local people wouldn't take in the visitors who came to see the ships off. She had travelled a long, long way, tramping and hitching rides on carts, desperate to be there before the *Lucy Collins* sailed. Now she sat up stiffly, wakened by the first rays of the sun, and huddled her shawl about her shoulders. Stiffly she clambered to her feet and went down to the water's edge to rinse the sleep from her eyes and shake the sand from her hair.

Her toilet made, she drew from her big basket a fresh dress. She had only worn it the once — the day before he was arrested. Now she must look her best for him so that he might remember her down the years ahead. Smoothing the dress down and tying a fresh ribbon in her hair, she hefted the big basket that held her last gifts to him and set off along the beach towards the jetty.

Hours later she stood on the jetty, her empty basket at her feet, watching the *Lucy Collins* turn across the harbour. The cold breeze was catching the ship's sails, flicking them grey and gold in the sunlight, and the outward bound flag — the Blue Peter — fluttered at the foremast head. She could see figures moving about the deck, but he was not among them. He would be down below in the darkened holds, not permitted even a last look at his native land, nor a farewell glimpse of his lover.

She snatched her shawl about her as the ship made for the open sea and tears streamed down her face. Unthinkingly she clasped in her right hand the small gift he had thrust into her fingers as the guards drove them apart. She did not know the sailor's superstition, that to watch a departing ship out of sight always brings grief, and if she had known it, she would still have watched because she already had all the grief in the world . . .

Sawney had stopped moaning and was looking at me expectantly. I came back to reality with a bump.

'Mr Sawney,' I said, 'I've told you what I think, that you won't even be charged. If you are, let me know and we'll see where it goes. Good afternoon.'

★ ★ ★

I always imagine the sailing of the *Lucy Collins* like that, but maybe I'm wrong. Maybe I see it like that because of what happened afterwards. Psychometrists believe that objects become steeped in the emotions that have surrounded them, and that these can be detected years and years later. Sometimes I wonder about that little piece of copper she clutched in her hand as she watched the *Lucy Collins* sail away. Was that why it brought us so much trouble a century and a half later?

I would never have heard of the *Lucy Collins* but for Sheila McKenna. My name is Tyroll, Chris Tyroll, solicitor of the Supreme Court by profession. The downside of the job is meeting people like Sawney. The upside is meeting a person like Sheila McKenna. She arrived in my office one day, having come from Australia to visit her only surviving relative. He happened to have been recently murdered, after which life for Sheila and me got dangerous and unpleasant.[1] At least once — when things were very unpleasant — she saved my life. It seems she saved it because she wanted it, which is very nice and explains why she was back in Britain on a year's sabbatical leave from the University of Adelaide, doing historical research for a book. That was what led her to the story of the *Lucy Collins*.

She sprang it on me over dinner at the Jubilee Room, which is the nearest thing my home town of Belston has to a good English restaurant. We were celebrating the end of the Walton and Grady case[2] when she took something out of her bag and passed it across the table.

It was an old-fashioned copper penny, beaten out flat and wide and with one side polished. On that side there was a decoration and some words.

'It came up for auction in London,' she said. 'As soon as I read about it I knew I had

---

[1] See *The Victory Snapshot*, Constable, 1997.

[2] See *Robbery With Malice*, Constable, 1999.

to have it. That's what I've been fixing up, raising some extra cash from the publishers and arranging for someone to bid for me, and there it is.'

She smiled triumphantly, and a triumphant smile from Sheila's grey eyes with their mask of freckles is something I'm normally prepared to wallow in but she had me puzzled.

'But what is it?' I said.

The smile turned to a frown. 'Come on, Tyroll. Use the grey matter. What does it look like?'

I looked at it again. 'It's a sailor's love token — a keepsake for his girlfriend.'

She shook her head firmly. 'This guy was going away for ever,' she said.

I strained to read the verse inscribed under the little decoration of a ship in full sail. It read:

Driven beyond all sight of your sweet
    face
By Lucy Collins harsh embrace
No more to gaze in your blue eyes
But labour under distant skies
Far from my hearts Desire for ever
Until we meet by Grace to dwell for
    Ever.

Underneath the verse were the initials 'JS', flanked by the words 'FOR EVER' and underneath that the date, 1865. A small hole had been punched in the top, piercing the ship's sails. From the smooth edges of the hole you could see that someone had carried it on a string or worn it around the neck.

'Who was Lucy Collins?' I asked.

'Not who — what!' she said. '*Lucy Collins* was a transport ship.'

The light dawned. 'And this was a convict's love token — not a sailor's?' I said. 'I never knew there were such things.'

She nodded. 'There are. They're usually earlier than that one but it's a good one, nevertheless. It's particularly good for my purposes.'

'How's that?'

'Well, my book is supposed to be about the convicts, right? Who they really were and so on, and now I've got something that one of them had made to leave with his wife or his girl. What's more, I've got the name of the ship and the year of sailing, and his initials. Almost all of the convict files are in the Public Records Office. I should be able to track him down.'

'How many times did the *Lucy Collins* sail to Oz in 1865?' I said. 'You may have to look at a number of voyages to find him.'

She shook her head. 'No,' she said. 'It was a four-month trip each way.'

'Four months!' I said. 'What about the tea-clippers? How fast were they?'

'*Cutty Sark* used to make Sydney Heads in about one hundred days out from London, but the *Lucy Collins* wouldn't have been built for speed. She'd have taken about four months. She'd only have made one trip in 1865. And that's another thing, it's not back in the Dark Ages — it's not even in the early days of transportation. It's near the end. It packed up a couple of years later. It's the mid-Victorian Empire with all its records — ship manifests, convict files, birth certificates, baptismal registers, log books, censuses — there'll be lots of material.'

I looked again at the medallion. 'JS?' I said. 'Pretty common initials, then and now. How many Jim Smiths or Jack Smiths were there on board your average convict transport? And apart from Smiths, S is a very common surname initial in England anyway.'

'Don't be a wowser,' she said. 'If I can locate the ship's convict manifest, I'll find out, won't I? Then I can try and trace where he came from and who the girl was — track down her descendants — maybe his descendants, if they had kids before he went. He might even have been one of the few that made it home again. There's a whole new chunk for my book in it — maybe a whole book, in fact. It may be a lot of yakka, but it'll be worth it.'

I grinned at her enthusiasm. 'OK,' I said. 'Even if there were a dozen JS's on the *Lucy Collins*, you'll be able to work out which one.'

'How?'

'Because the bloke who wrote that inscription must have been an engraver or something like that.'

'No marks,' she said. 'It was probably made for him by another convict — most probably a forger who was used to fine engraving. But don't you think it's a great idea?'

I did and I said so, and I really meant it, but if I'd known what was coming I'd have skimmed the damned thing out of the window.

2

It went all right at first. Sheila got stuck into her research with great enthusiasm and I went back to running a solicitor's office, that is worrying about clients and staff and whether the Legal Aid Board would pay before I went bust and so on. We didn't realise it at the time, but it all started to go wrong with what we called the 'Briefcase Incident'. We didn't catch on that the Briefcase Incident was more than peculiar — it meant something nasty.

Sheila's first target was the ship's sailing particulars. That was no problem. She soon knew that the *Lucy Collins* cleared from Portland, Dorset, in November 1865, with a cargo of convicts, bound for Fremantle, by Perth in West Australia. Next she went looking for a list of the convicts on board.

I recall her coming home from London one day with a photocopy of the Home Office warrant to the owners of the *Lucy Collins* to ship one hundred and forty-three convicts to Australia.

'Look!' she commanded, and pointed at

the list. 'James Simmonds. I told you I'd find him.'

'So you did, but is James Simmonds your JS? You've got John Smythe here, and a Jonty Sowden. There's a Jan Satton and a Jack Sullivan. That's five.'

'Great!' she said. 'I told you — I'll track all their families down and do a whole book about them.'

'You'll have to find out more than just their names,' I said.

'Sure, but there's about ninety-eight per cent of the convict files in the Public Records Office. The odds are on my side. And those files tell you where a bloke was sentenced. Never worry — I'll find them.'

I was still looking at the list. 'You'd better look for his file as well,' I said, pointing. 'Just because a Home Office clerk thought he spelled his name with a 'G' doesn't mean he did.'

'Gerry Sommers?' she said. 'OK, you might be right.'

She disappeared to London for a few days, to delve into the PRO files, but her evening phone calls told me she was finding what she wanted. When she came back she had a briefcase stuffed with photocopies.

After dinner she unloaded her case carefully on to the cleared dining-table, setting the copies out in six separate bundles.

'*Voilà!*' she announced. 'All six files of the JS's aboard the *Lucy Collins* in 1865.'

I picked up the top sheet of the first stack. It was the personal particulars of James Simmonds, written in a mixture of the beautiful regular hand of Victorian clerks and semi-literate scribbles.

'Why the difference?' I asked Sheila, pointing to the writing.

'There was always a shortage of educated labour,' she said. 'Any convict who could write at all could get himself a soft job as a clerk. I suppose the good bits are the professional clerks and the scribble is the convicts.'

I looked again at the details of James Simmonds and saw that he was a Midlander sentenced at Stafford Assizes. When I was first in articles the old Crown Court in the centre of Stafford was still in use and I must have been many times in the room where Jimmy Simmonds received his sentence. I read the record:

JAMES SIMMONDS No 2318
tried 24th July 1865,
arrived Fremantle Barracks March 1866.
Born 19th March 1843

Trade: None Height: 5 ft. 7 in.
Complexn: Fair Head: Large
Hair: Brown Whiskers: None
Visage: Broad Forehead: M.Ht
Eyebrows: Brown Eyes: Grey
Nose: Medium Mouth: Wide
Chin: Broad Remarks: Scar over
l.eyebrow, tattoo
r.forearm, Anchor &
HOPE on scroll.

Convict 7 years' transportation
Tried at Stafford, transported for robbery
Character: Bad

'This one was very short,' I remarked, thinking of him standing in the high old dock at Stafford.

'They all were. Rotten Pommy diet stunted them. The average height in these files is about five foot eight.'

The personal details were followed by sheet after sheet of a wearisome record of Simmonds' years in the penal colony — six years in all. He might have served much less with good behaviour, but the record didn't show good behaviour. It was an endless repetition of petty offences — 'having tobacco', for which he got a week's solitary confinement, 'improper possession of boots', another week in solitary, 'indecent behaviour in church', another week, 'assaulting fellow prisoner', twenty-five strokes.

'Was twenty-five strokes a bad flogging?' I asked.

'Well, I don't suppose it was much fun, but they used to give a lot more. They must have been going soft by this time. In the early days you read about two or three hundred lashes. Twenty-five was about the minimum. They used to call it a 'tester' or a 'Botany Bay dozen'. The guys who stood up to two or three hundred were called 'pebbles' or 'iron men'.'

The record went on — 'possessing turnips', 'singing in cell', 'indecency in cell' (probably the only pleasure they couldn't take away from him), each of which cost him seven days' solitary.

I looked through the other files. While James Simmonds was sent from Stafford Assizes, they were a mixed bunch geographically. John Smythe was sentenced at Winchester, Jan Satton at Bridgwater, Jonty Sowden at Shrewsbury, Jack Sullivan at Warwick and Gerry Somers at Oxford.

'You're lucky,' I remarked. 'Out of six,

16

you've got three Midlanders and one in Oxfordshire. That should cut down on your mileage a bit.'

'That's if they came from the towns where they were tried,' she said. 'They might have been strangers in the area, which'll make them hard to find. I thought, since I've got their birth-dates, that I'd try the Family Records Centre for birth certificates first. That might be a short cut and save me going through the trial records.'

3

Next evening I got home to find Buggalugs the cat rampaging around the kitchen door, howling for food. You might ask why we didn't have a cat-flap. Largely because — officially — we didn't have a cat.

My house is one of a number of villas built in Whiteway Village in the 1880s and '90s by local manufacturers, but at the bottom of the back garden a narrow lane divides the posh villas from the old craftsmen's workshops. The one immediately behind my gaff is a little brass-founder's shop where they knock out fake Victorian horse brasses and Boer War money-boxes and things. Buggalugs is their cat — or he was. One warm evening we left the kitchen door open to let the heat of cooking out. Suddenly we realised we were being observed by a little triangular black face with huge pointy ears. Sheila fed him, and there you are. All of a sudden he became her devoted slave.

'Listen,' I commanded him, as I filled a bowl with premium grade Rabbit and Steak cat-food, 'you used to subsist on bits of old sandwich from the brassworkers across the road and the odd fieldmouse or two. Don't get above your station, mate.'

He looked at me without expression and then tried to claw the dish out of my hands as I laid it on the back step.

Sheila came into the kitchen behind me. 'What's he done?' she asked.

'He's developing the idea that he's a middle-class cat, not a factory moggy,' I complained. 'It's your fault — all these Aussie ideas about equality.'

'He's not equal,' she said. 'He's a superior moggy. Those big pointy lugs are Egyptian. He could be the reincarnation of a priest of Bubastes.'

'Priests,' I said, 'are not supposed to be greedy and arrogant — they're supposed to be poor and humble and obedient.'

'Yair!' she said. 'Like the Pope and the Archbishop of Where-dyecallit, you mean? I take it you haven't had a good day?'

'Not so's you'd notice. Bad Penny turned up.'

'Who is Bad Penny?'

'Bad Penny,' I said, 'is properly known as Miss Penelope Wenton but is known to the entire legal profession of this area as Bad Penny.'

'Because she just turns up?'

'Precisely. And when she turns up she

always produces a carrier bag full of dog-eared photocopies and tells you that she wants you to prove that she's the rightful Countess of Warwick and has been cheated of her inheritance.'

'And is she? Has she?'

'Of course not! No — not 'of course not' — probably not, and anyway she can't prove it.'

'So what do you do?'

'Spend lots of wasted time explaining to her why all her photocopies won't prove she's the rightful Countess of Warwick. Then she comes over all Countessy and says you're no use and can you recommend a really good lawyer. Then you think of the colleague you like least and give her his address and off she goes. Then, months and months later, when you'd completely forgotten her up she pops again, some kindly colleague having given her your address and she having forgotten she's ever spoken to you.'

'Sounds fun. And could she be the Countess of Warwick?'

I shrugged. 'Who knows? Daisy Warwick put herself about a bit a century ago. She had a bad attack of Socialism and went bust and they say she tried to blackmail the Prince of Wales over some indiscreet letters. I wouldn't be the least bit surprised if there were unacknowledged Warwicks littering the country. We know there's lots of unacknowledged Royals.'

'Well then, why don't you prove her claim to the throne of England and make a fortune in fees?'

'Because the royal descent doesn't pass through the female side. I could only make her a Princess at best.'

'Bloody Pommy chauvinists,' she sneered.

'Hang on a bit! It was immigrants what did it. The British used to elect their kings. It was the Anglo-Saxon mob who changed the rules.'

'Don't try and weasel out of it by blaming it on the immigrants! I used to think Oz was a man's country, but they only learned it from you lot.'

'Have you had any luck at finding your convicts' girlfriends?' I said, changing the subject.

'Not bad,' she declared. 'I've found some of my convicts,' and she pulled a roll of photocopies from her shoulder-bag. 'See these?'

'You got their birth certificates?'

'Not all of them,' she said, 'but four out of six. Not bad, eh?' She grinned triumphantly and went in search of her briefcase.

I looked through the copies of birth records. 'What's the chance,' I called, 'of tracking these blokes down at the other end? In Australia?'

'About Buckley's,' she called back. She reappeared with her case. 'They usually changed their name once their sentence was over. You ever heard of Jim the Penman?'

'Of course,' I said. 'He was a lawyer and forger in the 1850s. He got himself transported.'

She nodded. 'That's right. He was pretty famous in his day. Because he kept his identity as Saward apart from his identity as Jim the Penman, the fuzz couldn't find him for years, sort of Jekyll and Hyde stunt. When they did lumber him it was big news — a prominent barrister going down for life. So he was shipped out and served his time as a convict. Then, when he was released into the Colony, he disappeared. No trace of him. That's what most of them did. That's why there's more chance of tracking the families this end.'

'Where did that token come from?' I asked. 'Wouldn't that help?'

She came back with her briefcase, shaking her head. 'No chance. It came out of a drawer in a London junkshop and he couldn't remember where he got it. Said it was probably in a house-clearance.'

I was still mulling over the copies of birth

certificates when an exclamation from Sheila made me look up. She had her briefcase open and was staring into it.

'My oath!' she said. 'I must be shickered.'

'I'd be sure you were,' I said, 'if I knew what it meant.'

'Drunk,' she snapped. 'You Pommy galah! If you're going to be the great love of my life, you'd better learn to talk Strine.'

'Right-o, cobber,' I said. 'Why are you shickered?'

Without a word she spun the briefcase around on the table and pushed it across to me. It seemed to be full of newspapers.

'Why'd you take a bag full of newspapers to London with you?'

'I didn't,' she said. 'This morning that case had the copies of the convict files in it.'

'You mean you've lost them? Some idiot's picked them up on the train?'

She shook her head. 'No. Luckily I scanned all the copies on to the computer and I made text copies as well to save reading all those different handwritings. I can print them out again. But look at this.'

She pushed the lid of the briefcase shut and pointed to three parallel scrape marks that slanted across the front.

'Mine had marks like that on it. This one's nearly identical.'

'Do you have any idea where it could have happened? Did you see anyone with this kind of briefcase?'

She shook her head again. 'Could have been on the train,' she said. 'It was pretty crowded and I was standing to Coventry.'

'You could ask at the station, but they charge an arm and a leg for lost property nowadays.'

'No point,' she said. 'My address is in the case. If the galah who took it wants his newspapers back, he'll get in touch.'

And we thought no more of it. Bad move. We should have wondered why someone took a case full of old newspapers to London.

4

It didn't take Sheila long to find the other two birth certificates at the Family Records Centre, once I'd reminded her that Satton was probably Sutton pronounced with a West Country accent and that Somers had several spellings.

Once she had them, she could back-track in the records for their parents, and after that came the publicity. Now she had some idea of the families that she was looking for, she needed publicity to help her find them. My computer-mad assistant, Alasdair, put her on the Internet and local television put her on screen, which was picked up by national TV and caught the eye of newspaper editors who don't actually publish pin-ups but aren't averse to stories with a beautiful woman in them.

All of which brought in tons of mail by post and e-mail. Almost every night we sat round after dinner and laughed our way through the bizarre letters that she received. Some of them were helpful, though, like one from a lady in Somerset:

Dear Miss McKenna

I was deeply interested to learn from our local newspaper that you are researching the family of a Jan Sutton who was transported to Western Australia in 1865.

I am by way of being an amateur genealogist, and have, for some years, been researching my family's past. Some of my ancestors were Suttons and lived in this area in the 1860s.

I now have an extensive collection of papers about my family and if you think there may be anything among them that will assist you, perhaps you would like to telephone and arrange a time when you could call and see them.

Yours sincerely, Dorothy Wainwright

By this time we had developed a filing system — six box files labelled 'Relevant', 'Interesting', 'Possible', 'Pointless', 'Boring' and 'Barking Mad'.

'Interesting,' I said and passed the letter across.

'More than interesting,' she said. 'Intelligent, well-educated, right area — Relevant, I think.'

'What's more,' I said, 'Sutton isn't a Somerset name. There shouldn't be many there. If she's got Suttons in her family tree she probably is some kind of relative to our Jan.'

Sheila reached for the phone. 'Don't come over all Australian at her,' I said. 'From the style of her letter she's probably elderly.'

I have seen Sheila shoulder-charge a man with a loaded gun and watched her kick a knife-wielding killer in the crotch but when she sets out to make herself agreeable to somebody she knows how to lay it on. She introduced herself on the phone in her poshest accent and, in minutes, she and Dorothy Wainwright were chatting like old pals.

She put the phone down, purring like a cream-fed cat. 'Doing anything Sunday?' she said.

'You know what we do on Sunday,' I said.

'Sure,' she said, 'but we'll have to leave it out if we're going to Norton Stavey.'

'Only if a) you drive there and back, and b) we can make up now for a lost Sunday morning.'

'Like how?'

'Like by dragging me off to bed and tearing my clothes off.'

'And then what?'

'You'll find instructions on the inside of my underpants if you can't remember.'

I was lying about that, but once we got that far she managed to remember from the time before.

5

Sunday started well enough, when Sheila and I agreed to renegotiate our agreement, but that made us a little late, so we pushed it down the M5.

Beyond Bridgwater we had to navigate through the back lanes of what they call the 'levels' to find Norton Stavey, a tiny hamlet near absolutely nowhere. Mrs Wainwright had told Sheila on the phone to look out for the one telegraph pole in the place, as it stood in her garden.

Sure enough, the telegraph pole stood in a garden which lay in front of a small, red-brick cottage, garden and house showing signs of long and loving care. As we drew up outside, the front door opened and a small, silver-haired woman in cream and brown came down the path to welcome us.

Soon we were seated in her front room, being pressed to make a choice from a tall cakestand loaded with crustless sandwiches of cucumber, egg and cress and a dozen other fillings. The crustless sandwiches went with the furniture, heavily flounced in vivid floral prints, and the diagonal lead strips on the windows to imitate seventeenth-century panes. Mrs Wainwright seemed to believe that she lived in a different Britain or to have a rose-tinted vision of the one she did occupy.

'I'm only a Wainwright by marriage,' she told us, when the refreshments had ended. 'My father was a Prust, but Mother had Sutton blood, and that's the family you're interested in, isn't it, Dr McKenna?'

Sheila explained her project, in more detail than she had on the phone, and produced the token from her shoulder-bag. Mrs Wainwright took it carefully, as though it were precious porcelain, and carried it to the window where she stood and examined it closely. Eventually she put it back into Sheila's hand just as carefully.

'How absolutely marvellous!' she said, her face shining. 'To hold an object with such a history fills one with awe. And so you believe, Dr McKenna, that there is a real possibility that the poor man who made that token was one of my ancestors?'

'I hope you may be able to tell us that, Mrs Wainwright. At the moment I know that six men with the initials JS sailed on the *Lucy Collins* and that one of them was a Jan or John Sutton.'

She drew from her shoulder-bag a copy of the convict file.

'We know that Jan Sutton was tried at Bridgwater, which is why we started looking in this area.'

She spread the papers on the coffee-table and Mrs Wainwright began to pore over them.

JAN SATTON No 7014
tried 17th July 1865,
arrived Fremantle Barracks March 1866.
Born 22nd April 1848

Trade: Farm labourer Height: 5 ft. 6 in.
Complexn: Dark Head: Small
Hair: Black Whiskers: None
Visage: Round Forehead: M.Ht
Eyebrows: Black Eyes: Black
Nose: Medium Mouth: Small
Chin: Small pointed Remarks: Scar on back
l.shoulder, tattoo
l.forearm heart and
MOTHER on scroll.
Convict 7 years' transportation
Tried at Bridgwater, transported for robbery
Character: Fair

Our hostess read every word, the description and all the long, miserable catalogue of petty offences punished by floggings and lockings-up.

'Poor man!' she exclaimed at last. 'Do you know anything else about him, Dr McKenna? Do you know the details of his trial?'

Sheila shook her head. 'I'm trying to find out about the men and their families before I get involved with what they were supposed to have done.' She reached into her capacious shoulder-bag again.

'Here's his birth certificate,' she said. 'This shows him born at Rendwary — '

'But that's only just up the road!' interrupted Mrs Wainwright. Sheila nodded. 'His parents were Mary Jane Thompson and Caleb Sutton, who is described as a farmer.'

Mrs Wainwright took the certificate and read it silently, but with a gleam of suppressed excitement in her eyes. When she had done she stood up.

'I do believe,' she said, 'that I can identify your John Sutton for you. Excuse me just one moment.'

She left the room but was very soon back bearing three large coloured loose-leaf folders. She deposited them on the coffee-table and selected the red one, laying it on her lap.

'These,' she said, 'are the fruits of my researches.'

'You must have been very busy,' I remarked. 'Those are thick files.'

She smiled. 'I started before I married, Mr

Tyroll. Then marriage and a child slowed me down, and I had a sick husband in his last years, but since my husband died I've really applied myself to it.'

She opened the file on her lap. 'Now,' she went on, 'you're looking for a John or Jan Sutton, born in Rendwary on 22nd April 1848 to Caleb Sutton and Mary Jane Thompson.'

'Right,' we both said simultaneously.

'Well,' she said, 'my records show that he was the youngest of four brothers, Matthew, Mark, Luke and John, born in 1842, 1845, 1847 and 1848 respectively.'

Sheila and I looked at each other, amazed. 'You're sure?' asked Sheila.

'Almost entirely certain,' Mrs Wainwright replied. 'You see, we have family records of him but I never could learn exactly what happened to him. Let me show you.'

She reached for a blue folder and turned the plastic-covered pages in it, stopping at last at a photocopy.

'There,' she said. 'That's the flyleaf of a family Bible that my cousins own.'

The entries read:

Matthew Sutton
    14th May 1842
        Murdered in Arizona, 1884

Mark Sutton
  12th March 1845
    26th November 1910 (never wed)
Luke Sutton
  9th August 1847
    Married Elizabeth Smith 1865
    Died 23rd October 1901
John Sutton
  22nd April 1848
    Married Maud Barton, 1864
    Daughter Mary Jane born 1865
    John lost at sea in passage to Australia
    1865

When we looked up she was smiling at us.

'Mary Jane Sutton,' she said, 'was my great-grandmother. She was brought up with Luke's family and married one of their Smith cousins. Her daughter, Elizabeth Smith, was my grandmother. She lived till 1956 and I recall her well.' She showed us a diagram in the first folder, setting out that side of her family tree and continuing down to her own son, Norman, and his three children.

'So you see,' she said, triumphantly, 'you've solved a little mystery for me. Now I know what became of my great-great-grandfather.'

'Excuse me a moment,' I said. 'I'm sure you've been very careful in your research, Mrs Wainwright, but that Bible note says

Sutton died at sea.'

She nodded. 'Oh, I've known there was something peculiar about him. You see that entry about his marriage to Maud Barton? I've searched and searched in the records and never found that marriage and that's because there wasn't one. What I have found in the County Records was censuses in 1851 and 1861 showing a Maud Barton in Rendwary. She'd have been the right age to be his sweetheart, but she's still there in 1871 as an unmarried woman. Then she disappears.'

Sheila nodded thoughtfully. 'So John Sutton left Maud Barton pregnant when he got into his trouble . . . '

'And his family took his child in,' said Mrs Wainwright, 'and someone wrote that note in the Bible to tidy up all the loose ends. There's no illegitimate girl there and no son convicted of robbery.'

She seemed completely unflustered by the news that her ancestry was illegitimate, and I was about to ask her about the bloke who was murdered in Arizona when a car drew up noisily outside.

She glanced out of the window. 'Here's my son, Norman,' she said. 'He'll be so pleased to meet you. He's always taken an interest in my genealogical researches.'

She went to the front door and shortly we

were introduced to Norman, a chubby, balding man in his forties who didn't seem very pleased to meet us. In fact he seemed vaguely distracted while we were introduced. We explained our errand and he nodded without comment, then excused himself and his mother and drew her into the hall.

While the family discussion went on in the hall, Sheila and I leafed through Mrs Wainwright's fat file-folders, but she was back quite quickly. Norman was not with her and we heard his car drive away.

Our hostess seemed a little flustered. 'I'm afraid Norman can't stay,' she said. 'He's on his way to Bristol on business. Let me get you some more tea.'

She returned from the kitchen more composed and I asked my question. 'What happened to Matthew Sutton — the eldest brother who was murdered in Arizona? That seems a strange end for a lad from a West Country farm.'

She smiled. 'I think old Caleb thought that naming his sons after the Evangelists would make them saintly,' she said, 'but it didn't seem to work. John you know about. Mark was a drinker and a wastrel by all accounts. Luke was the one who married and settled down and worked the farm. Matthew went to America when he was young. He fought in their Civil War.'

She leaned over and leafed through one of her folders, turning it to show us when she found the right page. In the plastic pocket was a photograph of a short dark man with heavy whiskers. He wore the uniform of the Confederate States Army.

'That's Matthew,' she said. 'He sent that picture home.' She turned the page to another photograph, a faded Victorian group. 'He came home afterwards,' she said, 'and that's him with his parents and his brothers — apart from poor John, of course.'

The men in the photograph all resembled the description of John Sutton in his convict record.

'But he went back again?' I asked.

'Oh yes. He couldn't settle here, so he went back. He went prospecting and they say he made a good deal of money, but he was killed in Arizona.'

'Murdered, according to your family Bible,' commented Sheila.

'Well, yes, but it wasn't what you might call a personal murder. He and his companions were attacked by Red Indians and most of them were killed. Would a copy of that family photograph be a help to you, Dr McKenna?'

'Marvellous,' smiled Sheila. 'I hardly dared to ask.'

'Oh, you can have copies of anything I've got,' Mrs Wainwright said. 'It's been so exciting to find out about poor John and to see your wonderful penny. Do you think that John might have given that to Maud Barton, Dr McKenna?'

'It's certainly a possibility. It's great to know that he had a sweetheart and to know her name, Mrs Wainwright, but it's too early to say if she was the lady it was made for.'

'Well, until you prove otherwise, I shall choose to believe that she was. Now, I know you haven't had much time to look at all my papers, but I've got most of them on computer and I've made you a copy of the disk.'

She went out again and I blinked at the thought of Mrs Wainwright being computer-literate. She was back in a second with a floppy disk.

'There you are,' she told Sheila. 'There's all the family tree there, scanned-in photographs, extracts from news cuttings and so on, but if there's anything else you need do please ask. Now I shall start looking for the record of his trial. That'll be something new and interesting.'

Sheila grinned broadly. 'It looks like you've done most of my work on the Sutton family, Mrs Wainwright. I don't know how to thank you and I'll certainly see you get an acknowledgement, but there is one more thing — the farm where John was born. Is it still standing?'

'Oh yes. It's only about four miles from here. It's not in the family now, but it's still there.'

She gave us complete directions for finding the farm and we parted very amicably.

6

'Bonzer!' exclaimed Sheila as we pulled away from Mrs Wainwright's cottage. 'That little lady has saved me almost a sixth of my research and actually identified someone who might have been the girl the token was made for.'

'Not to mention selling umpteen copies of your book to the whole of her enormous clan,' I remarked.

'Why's that?'

'Because, my love, I had a look at the folder Mrs W didn't show us while she was outside having a barney with Norman.'

'And what's in it?'

'Notes about the Confederate ancestor, whatsisname — Matthew.'

'But she didn't seem to know a great deal about him, apart from the fact that the Indians got him and his pals.'

'Ah, but she did say that he was supposed to have made a lot of money.'

'Don't tell me! He found the Lost Dutchman Mine and then lost it again?'

'Not quite. The notes suggest that he didn't just come back to England once after the

Civil War, he came at least twice. The second time was after one of his prospecting trips. Apparently they believe that he brought a load of gold and deposited it in the Bank of England.'

She snorted. 'Another secret deposit in the Bank of England! Like the Romanov's gold and the pirate fortune that three thousand people in Cuba think is in there!'

'Maybe,' I said, 'but she seems to believe it.'

'And that's what Norman was going troppo about,' she said.

'How do you know?'

'Sharp ears, mate. Raised in the bush, you've got to have sharp ears.'

'You weren't raised in the bush — you said you went to a posh school in Adelaide run by nuns!'

'Same thing, mate. When you're smoking in the dunny you've got to be able to hear a wimple rustle at a hundred yards.'

'So what did you hear?'

'Norman wanted to know what she'd told us and she said she hadn't told us about Matthew. He said she shouldn't have had anything to do with us. She said we might be useful, that we'd already eliminated any claim by the Bartons.'

'So she knew at least something about the

Bartons already, then.'

'Well, she told us she couldn't find John's supposed marriage and she'd guessed that the Bible entry was a fake to put people off the trail.'

I laughed. 'I'll bet old Caleb wrote that. Any man who names his four sons after the Evangelists has got to be the kind of pious fraud who'd write lies in his Bible.'

'Do you think he was trying to cover up or trying to give the illegitimate line a chance at the money?'

'I don't think they had one anyway. If Matthew died intestate — and we lawyers are always warning people to make wills in good time, not to leave it till you're holed up in a cave in Arizona with the entire Apache nation outside wanting to decorate their wigwams with you — then his brothers were his heirs and after that their legitimate issue. I suspect that, even if there were a pile of gold in the Bank, the Wainwright's aren't in line for it.'

We found the old Sutton farm and photographed it, then made our way back to the motorway. I pointed out to Sheila the church with a weathercock that's supposed to crow.

'Yair,' she said. 'Pull the other one!'

'No, seriously. It's supposed to be specially constructed so that when the wind blows from a particular direction it crows.'

'Travelling with you, Chris Tyroll, is amazing. Remember when you told me about those two tramps who murdered their mate in the garbo heap on the M1?'

'If you don't want informed comment, you have only to say so. By the way, we're coming to a Services.'

'You want to point your Percy?'

'Not really. It's just that Mrs W's crustless sarnies have worn off and I'm starving.'

She grinned. 'Why do people cut the crust off?'

'Don't ask me. I suppose they think it's daintier.'

'Daintier!' Sheila snorted. 'Then they fill them with egg and cucumbers to give you the farts!'

On a fine Sunday evening in early summer the Services were busy. It was over an hour before we came out on to the car-park. Sheila's car was gone. Definitely. We searched the car-park, but it was gone, stolen. So it was statements to the police, a cab into Bristol and two hours on the train and another cab to get home. A rotten ending to a nice, successful day, but don't believe people who tell you that things can't get worse. They always can.

By the time we made it home we were both

tired and irritable. I started upstairs. Sheila turned back, saying that she was going to feed Buggalugs.

'He's quite fat enough. One night without an extra meal won't kill him.'

'Don't take it out on the poor moggy,' she said. 'He didn't duff the car!'

I was trudging on upstairs making my mind up to have Monday morning off, when Sheila called me from the kitchen.

She was standing by the kitchen table in the dark, looking at a sheet of paper by the light from the passage. As I came in she handed it to me.

'It was slipped under the door,' she said in a puzzled tone. 'What's it mean?'

It was a sheet of white, ordinary A4 size, with a couple of lines of text printed across the middle:

DR MCKENNA — THERE ARE MORE WAYS THAN CHOKING WITH CREAM

Sheila made for the back door while I stared at it. If I hadn't been tired I might have been quicker, but it took a moment to dawn.

'It's a proverb,' I said. ' 'There are more ways . . . ' '

I broke off and leapt across the room but I was too late. Sheila had opened the back door and snapped the light on. As I reached her, I heard her choked gasp of dismay, then she turned quickly towards me, burying her face in my shoulder, panting and cursing under her breath. Behind her I could see the pool of bright, fresh blood glistening on the pale stone. Buggalugs lay on the back step in a pool of his own blood. His throat was cut right across. Another sheet of paper lay on top on his little black body.

I pushed Sheila into a chair, snatched the second paper and slammed the door, throwing the bolt and snapping the outside light off. Then I poured us both a large whisky.

We drank in silence. Sheila sat with her head hung down. When she reached the bottom of the glass she just reached out and poured another. I followed her.

At length she looked up. Her face was white, making her mask of freckles into stark bands around her wide, wet eyes.

'What the hell . . . ' she began.

'It's a threat,' I said. I had read the second message. 'The paper slipped under the door was the first part. It's a proverb — 'There are more ways of killing a cat than choking it with cream'.' I showed her the second paper's text:

CURIOSITY IS A FAMOUS WAY.

'Curiosity killed the cat', she recited dully, then her anger sparked. 'It wasn't bloody curiosity! It was some sicko who wanted to frighten me, so he killed that poor little moggy!'

She gave vent to an incomprehensible snarl of rage, balled up both papers and flung them across the room.

Afterwards we lay in bed, having made love with the intensity that only those sickened by blood and frightened by death can achieve. Tiredness notwithstanding, neither of us slept. I was smoking silently, hoping that Sheila had fallen asleep, when she spoke.

'I've been thinking,' she said, 'about the Briefcase Incident.'

'So have I,' I said, 'and your car.'

'You mean the car was part of it?'

'Your briefcase was on the back seat.'

'But it was the other case — the one with the newspapers in it. If he thought he was getting anything worthwhile he blew it. Mrs W's disk is in my shoulder-bag.'

'Fine, but he probably pinched the car to make sure that whoever did it had time to get here ahead of us, suss the situation out, do his dirty work and get clear away.'

'But who? Why?'

'Who I don't know. Why is pretty plain from the notes. Somebody doesn't want you looking into their family history.'

'But if it started with the briefcase — I hadn't advertised what I was doing then.'

'No, but you were at the Family Records Centre, no doubt using certain years' registers only. Maybe he was there, using those same registers, noticed you were using them and got to wonder what you were up to.'

'But how would he find out before it was publicised?'

'He couldn't. That's why he needed to prepare a briefcase as near as dammit like yours, follow you and swap them over, so that he got your files. I should have realised that nobody walks about with a case full of old newspapers.'

'But what does he want?'

'I thought he'd made that pretty clear — he wants you to stop.'

There was a long silence.

'What do you think I should do?' she asked, at length.

'I'm not going to advise you to stop. You wouldn't take any notice anyway. But you need to be careful — very careful. So far he's killed a cat, but people who hurt animals often end up hurting people. He's unbalanced and he's violent.'

'No, I'm not going to stop. I'm damned if I

will. But who is it?'

'It could be anybody. The only half-way reasonable suspect at the moment is chubby Norman.'

'Norman Wainwright? You mean . . . '

'I mean that Norman and his mum seem to think there's gold about somewhere. He didn't want his mother to have anything to do with us. Perhaps he's decided to act alone.'

'But, if the Wainwrights are chasing old Matthew's gold, I've given them new information and new traces, surely.'

'You've shown them that there's quite possibly an Australian branch of the family — and you're Australian.'

'You mean he thinks I'm Cousin Sheila blown in from Oz to scoop the pool! He'd have to be crazy!'

'Whoever killed Buggalugs was crazy, Sheila. Be careful.'

She rolled half on top of me and pressed her face against my shoulder. 'I'm not going to stop,' she said, drowsily, and fell asleep.

7

In the morning I phoned John Parry, an old friend and a good one. The big Welshman is a detective inspector at Belston nick. John is a bachelor for the second time around and the promise of a good meal will always draw him.

Over lunch we told him the whole story and showed him the notes.

'Laser printed,' he mused. 'Properly spelled. Not your average illiterate animal mutilator. Who knew you were in Somerset?'

'Nobody,' I said. 'That's why we thought of chubby Norman.'

'Huh,' he said. 'Well, I can't have chubby Norman taken into Bridgwater nick and sweated just because someone's killed a cat in the Midlands.'

He looked evenly at Sheila. 'I suppose there's not a chance that you'd . . . '

'No,' she said. 'There isn't and I wouldn't't!'

He drew a deep breath. 'Ah, well,' he said, 'having made the serious mistake of trying to stop you before, I shan't push that

49

suggestion any further. I would remind you, however, that in the past you and Chris have shown a regrettable tendency to trip over corpses rather larger than cats. I'd be grateful if you'd try and limit that aspect of the matter — or at least find them on someone else's patch.'

'I'm not terribly concerned about other people's bodies,' I said. 'Only this one,' and I laid an arm on Sheila's shoulder.

He nodded. 'Same advice as I've given you before, boyo — and you've both ignored before — be very careful. Try not to be alone and be cautious about where you go and who you deal with. In the meantime I'll see if I can think of an excuse for asking Somerset and Avon to find out where chubby Norman was last evening.'

When he had gone, I removed Buggalugs' remains from the doorstep and washed down the stone. I laid the cat to rest in a corner of the garden, a shady place behind the shrubs where he used to loll about on warm afternoons. I didn't say a prayer over him, but I did mutter a curse on the psychopathic swine who'd killed him.

When I got back, Sheila was in the kitchen. 'That was pretty pointless,' she said.

'Oh, come on, Sheila. You knew that John

couldn't turn out the entire Central Midlands force over a dead cat. At least he'll keep some kind of an eye on chubby Norman.'

'Huh!' she snorted and went off to her computer.

She was back in minutes. 'I've got an e-mail about another of my convicts,' and she passed me a printout.

A dealer in prints at Winchester had picked up her enquiries on the Internet and thought he had information. He had sold a Victorian broadsheet about John Smythe to a local man who claimed to be descended from Smythe. Would Sheila like to be put in touch?

There was a graphics file attached to his e-mail. Once Sheila had unravelled it, she printed it out.

'That's crazy!' she exclaimed, as the sheet emerged from the printer. 'It's the wrong man!'

She showed me the print, a copy of a fairly ordinary Victorian broadside. It was headed, 'The Execution of John Smythe who was sentenced at Winchester Assizes'.

'But he was transported,' I said.

'That's why he's got the wrong man,' she said. 'And I was all enthusiastic, e-mailed him back to put me in touch with his client.'

'Where did your John Smythe come from?'
I asked.

She got out her copy of the convict file.
'Well, that's very odd,' and she pointed.

JOHN SMYTHE No 7229
tried 22nd July 1865,
arrived Fremantle Barracks March 1866.
Born 21 February 1843

Trade: Printer

Complexn: Fair	Height: 5 ft. 8 in.
Hair: Brown	Head: Small
Visage: Long	Whiskers: Moustache
Eyebrows: Brown	Forehead: High
Nose: Medium	Eyes: Brown
Chin: rounded	Mouth: Wide
	Remarks: Scar on back
	l.hand, No tattoos.
	Horiz. scar on r.ribs

Convict life transportation
Tried at Winchester, transported for robbery
Character: Good

'Look,' she said. 'This character was a printer
as well and he was tried at Winchester five
days before the bloke in the broadside was
hanged.'

THE EXECUTION OF
JOHN SMYTHE

WHO WAS SENTENCED AT WINCHESTER ASSIZES FOR THE MURDER OF

ALBERT LARNER

With Full Particulars of the Condemned Man's Last Dying Speech

At Winchester Assizes last week John Smythe, a printer of Wherwell, was placed before the bar charged with the murder of Albert Larner an apprentice in the same printing works. Evidence was given that Mr Ingram, the printer, had left the two together on a night in May to complete an urgent piece of work. Returning in the morning he found Larner killed with a maul and Smythe absent. A telegraph message led to the murderer's apprehension at Southampton railway station. Before Mr Justice Fotheringhay the prisoner pleaded Not Guilty, saying that Larner had been drunk and had attacked him so that in defending himself he had been forced to kill the youth, but he was able to call no witness in his defence and was found Guilty.

On July 27th he was hanged at Winchester Gaol before a crowd of some ten thousand, walking to the gallows with a firm step and thanking the Chaplain and Mr Calcraft.

Before being launched into eternity he said, 'You see the effects of strong drink, that has taken the lives of two of us.'

★★★★★★★★★★

Ingram, Printer, Parchment Street.

'Where did your Smythe come from? Where was he born?'

She dug the copy birth certificate out of her folder. 'Well I'm damned!' she said. 'Wherwell! Same as the bloke in the broadside.'

'Wherwell's a tiny place now,' I said. 'There can't have been all that many John Smythe's in it — all working for printers. You're going to have to look at the Hampshire County Census returns for 1861 and 1871 to see if you can sort these two out.'

She shook her head slowly. 'It doesn't make any kind of sense.' She read the broadside copy again. 'What's a maul?'

'It's a wooden mallet. Letterpress printers used to use them for tapping the type down level on the bed of the big old presses.'

'Who was Mr Calcraft?' she asked.

'He was the public hangman for years and years — well, one of them. Probably the most famous. He got taken to court himself for failing to support his aged mother and letting her become a charge on the parish. There was a broadside about that and afterwards the crowds at executions used to rag him about it and call out, 'Who starved his mother, Billy?' '

'Do you know the history of every obscure crime in Britain?' she asked.

'Not really. I just had a misspent youth. My mother had a collection of old books on crime, things like *Mysteries of Police and Crime* and *Lives of the Great Highwaymen*. I couldn't get enough of them. That's how I ended up a penniless criminal lawyer, instead of a fat cat in company and property law.'

The phone rang and Sheila went to answer it. She came back smiling. 'Fancy a trip to Winchester?' she said.

'Why? Who was that?'

'That was Captain Smythe, retired — the man who bought the broadside. He's heard from the dealer and he rang up straightaway.'

'So, did you tell him he's descended from the wrong murderer?'

'I tried to, but he wouldn't have it. Said he could explain all that if I fancied travelling all the way to Hampshire.'

'Beware,' I said, 'of ex-officers who use their rank in civilian life. A rough colonial like yourself wouldn't appreciate the social subtlety, but pukka chaps don't do it — only self-aggrandising twits whose greatest moment of glory was commanding the gascape store at Little Wittering in 1962.'

'You could be right,' she admitted. 'He sounded a bit like that — all bluff and hearty — but nevertheless I've told him that I'd be delighted to travel all the way to Hampshire.'

'We will travel all the way to Hampshire,' I said. 'You are not going anywhere alone at present let alone into the clutches of some military nutter who's been trained at vast expense to kill with a bent spoon. Best police advice. You know it makes sense.'

'Trouble is, we don't have a car.'

'There's trains from Brum to Winchester. Anyway, at least it means that chubby Norman can't steal it again.'

In the event we booked a long weekend, travelling by train on Friday, having fixed an appointment with Captain Smythe for lunch on Sunday. We spent Friday evening and Saturday doing touristy things in Winchester, seeing the cathedral, having a pint in the oldest pub in England, viewing the several military museums and standing in the hall of the castle, where King Arthur's fake Round Table hangs.

'Should interest you, this place,' I told her. 'A measurable percentage of the kids you grew up with probably had ancestors who were sentenced here.'

'Really?' she said.

'Really. In 1832 — after the agricultural riots — they sat a Special Commission here that handed out a hundred death sentences and six hundred sentences of transportation.'

'My oath! A hundred for death and six hundred transports?'

'That's right, but they came over all merciful and remitted all but six of the capital sentences. They transported them instead.'

'Wonderful,' she said. 'What made them change their minds?'

'There was a bit of a fuss about the fact that only one person was killed in the riots and that was a bystander who got accidentally shot by a soldier.'

Sunday morning, after a leisurely breakfast, we took a cab out along the Petersfield road, following Captain Smythe's explicit directions. Half-way along the Meon valley we turned aside from the main road, climbed a hill and wove along some narrow, sunken lanes. At last we spotted an unpretentious wooden fingerpost pointing to Greyhanger

Farm, the address we had.

Greyhanger Farm was not my idea of a farm and its fingerpost was the only unpretentious thing about it. It was a gem of an eighteenth-century manor house, surrounded by immaculate lawns and stately old trees. Captain Smythe had evidently heard us coming and was waiting at the door, a tall, broad man with short grey hair and a military moustache, clad in cavalry twill slacks and a discreetly checked shirt with what I guessed to be the regimental tie.

'Ah,' he roared at Sheila, in that false hearty accent that seems to go with retained military ranks. 'The little lady from Australia, and this'll be your fiancé. Come in, come in!'

Once inside a hall set about with antique furniture (or at least good fakes), we were introduced in turn to Mrs Smythe (small, vague, tweedy and over-pearled), daughter Jennifer (twentyish, tall, blonde, attractive, posh accent) and son Simon (seventeen, fair, public school accent).

'Jenny's in television at Southampton,' explained our host, 'Simon's still at school and my wife devotes her time to good works.'

'And this is all your family?' asked Sheila.

'Well, there's Stephen — he lives and works in London, can't be here. He's something arty, graphic designer or something.'

'And what do you do, Captain?' I asked.

'Retired from investment consultancy,' he said. 'Though I still place a bit of money here and there for chums. If you've got a few bob spare it's my job to know where to put it. You're a lawyer, aren't you? Bet you chaps don't go short of the readies.'

'We do at my end of the market,' I said. 'Contrary to proverbial wisdom, crime doesn't pay.'

He laughed. 'So you're in the crime business,' he said. 'Which brings us back to business. The wife'll rustle up a drink or two while I show you the original of that broadside about John Smythe and I can explain what's bothering you, my dear.'

People who address Sheila McKenna as 'little lady' and 'my dear' are risking getting bitten, but she only glowered slightly while our host ushered us into his study, a large room facing across the lawn at the rear of the house to well-kept flower beds.

One wall of the study was hung from waist to ceiling in framed prints, documents and photographs. Many of the photographs were military men and several of them were Smythe himself. Once his wife had served drinks, Captain Smythe lifted down a frame.

'There it is,' he said, 'the broadside about the hanging of John Smythe.'

'Yet you say he wasn't hanged,' said Sheila.

'Quite right, my dear. There's no doubt at all that you are right in your original information. John Smythe was shipped to Fremantle on the *Lucy Collins*.'

'His sentence was commuted?' I suggested.

'Exactly! You see it says here that he said he had bashed Larner in self-defence. Well, after the sentence, people came forward who could testify that Larner had a bit of a reputation as a drunken lout. Smythe's family weren't entirely stony and they'd got a half-way decent lawyer, so he rushed about a bit, petitioned the Home Secretary and the sentence was commuted to transportation for life.'

Sheila nodded. 'I see,' she said, 'and you are sure that this John Smythe was the same one that sailed on the *Lucy Collins*?'

'What's your chappie's date of birth?' he asked, reaching into a drawer of his desk.

'21st February 1843, at Wherwell in Hampshire, son of Martha Smythe formerly Fray and James Smythe, coach-builder,' she recited, fumbling through her shoulder-bag for the copy.

'Snap!' he said as they both produced birth certificates which were identical.

We all laughed. 'Right-o,' conceded Sheila. 'He really is the same bloke. So how do we have here an account of his hanging 'With Full Particulars of the Condemned Man's Last Dying Speech'?'

'Because,' I intervened, 'his boss, Mr Ingram the printer, saw an opportunity when his assistant was sentenced to the drop, and knocked out a broadsheet for the patterers to sell at the occasion. But those sheets had to be hot news, didn't they? You couldn't note the real scene and print the sheet up afterwards, so you imagined it and printed it up a day or so before, sold it to the patterers who hawked them at the execution and on the streets and cleaned up very nicely. I think the patterers' expression was 'pretty tidy browns' for a lot of pennies and half-pennies made selling a good sheet. Do you know that some sheets sold in the hundreds of thousands and a few topped a million?'

'Exactly!' said Smythe. 'Poor old Ingram must have been really dis-chuffed when John was reprieved, unless he'd already unloaded his stock on to the patterers. That's why I wanted that sheet when I was told about it. Had to add that to my collection. Damned good joke, I thought. People come in here and see it and they ask me what relation of mine he was. You should see their faces when I tell them!'

'What was the relationship?' asked Sheila.

'He was my great-grandfather, that's what he was.'

'So he married before he was transported?' said Sheila, obviously looking for a candidate for recipient of the token.

Smythe shook his head and grinned. 'Oh no,' he said. 'Much more complicated than that. Tell you all about it over lunch.'

He ushered us into the dining-room and we settled into one of those traditional English roast-beef Sunday lunches that are wonderful in winter and absolute hell on a scorching summer's day. There was no dodging the column, though. From either end of the table the Captain and his wife pressed further helpings on us until I thought I would split down the middle. Sheila, on the other hand, was shaming me by putting it down like a navvy. It must be all those steak and egg breakfasts they eat.

Apart from the weight of the meal, we were further burdened by Captain Smythe's reminiscences. Born in 1940, he had managed to miss World War Two and Korea and had enjoyed an entirely safe military career that, if he was to be believed, had consisted almost entirely of jolly, drunken escapades in Hong Kong, Singapore and the Persian Gulf.

He paused only when the food was cleared

to suggest, 'Coffee and a spot of something stronger on the terrace.'

The stone-flagged terrace looked out across a large, well-kept garden and would have been a pleasant place to be on a hot day in other company. With the drinks, Mrs Smythe produced the family albums, releasing a new torrent from her husband, though this time at least some of it was relevant to Sheila's interests.

'You wanted to know about old John's marriage,' he said to Sheila and showed her a page of an album.

It was a late Victorian or Edwardian family group — a solidly built man in his sixties, a younger wife holding a baby, a youth of about twenty in uniform, a teenage boy and a toddler. The resemblance of the father to Captain Smythe was evident.

'That was taken,' he told us, 'when Great-Uncle John came home from South Africa after the Boer do. That's him in the uniform, his brothers, James and Arthur, and the baby's Great-Aunt Alice. She only died in 1986. Lovely old dear, sharp as a tack right to the end.'

'That wasn't what you used to say when she was alive,' his wife murmured.

'Well, she could be a bit demanding, but she was a game old girl.'

63

'So the father in this group is the John Smythe who wasn't hanged?' said Sheila.

'Exactly!' said Smythe. 'He was sentenced to life, of course, and should have ended his days in Australia, but he was a useful sort of chappie. When he got out there he realised that an educated man who was also a skilled printer was useful and could make favours for himself. So when he'd done his convict term, as a prisoner, he started a business and, after a few years, he managed to get his sentence remitted so that he could come home.'

'And that was when he married? After he came back?' asked Sheila.

'No, my dear. He brought her back with him. As you can see, she was a deal younger than him, and their last child — that's Great-Aunt Alice in the photo there — was born in 1900.'

He told us how his great-uncle John had stayed in the army after South Africa and had died in the Great War. His brothers, James and Arthur, had served in the war too, but only James had survived.

'He had only one son,' he explained. 'Another John. That's him in this picture.'

The photograph showed a World War Two captain with a baby on his knee.

'And the baby's me. That's me and my father. I was born just after the war started and that's us the first time we met.'

'Did he survive the war?' I asked.

'Oh, yes. Made Colonel by the end. Died the same year as old Alice, 1986. So you see, we've become a military dynasty. If they'd topped old John at Winchester the country would have lost some good fighting men.'

The warm afternoon wore on and the combination of Smythe's reminiscences and repeatedly refreshed drinks turned it into a sunny blur for me. Pressed to stay for tea we couldn't manage a convincing excuse for refusal but managed to break away afterwards with only a final visit to the display of pictures in the study. As we climbed into our cab, Smythe was warmly promising Sheila every co-operation and copies of any pictures she wanted.

By the time we were on a train out of Winchester the alcohol had begun to wear off and I started to take notice. Sheila, sitting opposite, was scribbling notes.

'You're not trying,' I said, 'to get down all of Smythe's ramblings, are you?'

'Only the essentials,' she said. 'He's promised to send me a family tree and anything I want. I thought the bit about the book was good.'

'What bit about the book?'

'I thought you were shickered,' she said.

'Smythe said that old John — my man, right? — when he came home went back into printing and in his old age he wrote a book about his experiences. Apparently it was called *A Victim of the System* and he printed it himself.'

'And hasn't Smythe got a copy?'

'Yes, but it's in London, being rebound. He'll let me see it when it's available.'

'Great stuff,' I said. 'When you started out on this I thought it was going to be pretty difficult, but so far it's been fairly easy.'

'So far,' she said. 'But it's only two out of six. I haven't any more info on the other four, so the hard bit may be ahead.'

It was long dark when we arrived home. I was picking up our bags after paying off the cab when the recollection of our homecoming from Somerset returned with a jolt. I carried the luggage inside and left Sheila in the sitting-room while I surveyed the ground floor. Nothing seemed out of place and a quick look out of the kitchen door revealed no more nasty surprises. Nevertheless, I was still uneasy.

While Sheila brewed coffee, I slipped out into the garden and sneaked round the edges, peering into the shadows. Finding nothing, I went out by the rear gate into the lane behind and came back along the dark walled alley that runs along one side of my premises. That place is as black as a coal-cellar at midnight and I walked through it pumping so much adrenalin that I was fully sober before I emerged.

When I came out I startled an old man whose dog was peeing against the lamp-post outside my gate. He jumped at my appearance and dragged his still-leaking dog away. I called 'Goodnight' but all I got was an unintelligible mutter from under his thick white moustache. I guessed that my paranoia had become infectious at a distance. But it's not paranoia when they really are after you, is it?

8

A long weekend usually means a long day's catching-up at the office afterwards, and Monday was just that. When I'd finally lowered the In-tray to a respectable level and was just about to leave, the phone rang. I was tempted to leave it and let the answering machine tell whoever it was that the office was closed and emergency calls could be made to whichever of my staff was on duty that night. I knew it wasn't me.

Conscience won. I have this feeling that if I'd been arrested and locked up (and I have been) I wouldn't like my loved ones listening to answering machines when they went looking for assistance, so I picked it up.

As it happened it was John Parry. 'Thought I'd catch you there,' he said. 'Why do you sit at your desk on a summer evening when you've got a beautiful Australian girl waiting for you at home?'

'Partly because I have to make a living and partly because I know that she isn't waiting for me — she's sitting in front of her computer playing Waltzing Matilda round the Internet.'

'Well, just remember that I warned you not to let her be alone, boyo.'

'Is this just our friendly neighbourhood Voice of Doom calling, or was there a reason?'

'Not much of a reason, but I thought you ought to know.'

'To know what?'

'That I had Somerset and Avon check out Norman Wainwright. I checked his car registration and gave it to them, saying we'd got a hit and run in the Midlands and that might be the car. Asked them to find out where he was on that Sunday evening.'

'And where was he?'

'In the arms of the Lord, boyo.'

'You mean he's snuffed it?'

'No, no. Merely that he was in Bristol, at a Spiritualist meeting, that's all. Got a whole load of respectable old biddies of both sexes to vouch for him. So he's not your cat-killer.'

'Never struck me as the spiritual type — but then one of his ancestors named his four sons Matthew, Mark, Luke and John, and wrote lies in the front of the family Bible to cover up a bastard child. That's your religious types for you.'

'Have a care, bach. You're talking to a son of the chapel. Any more of that and I'll come round and sing Cwm Rhondda under your windows all night.'

I thanked John for his efforts and told him that we'd had no further manifestations.

On the way home I thought about chubby Norman at a Spiritualist meeting. Then it dawned on me — the greedy little berk was probably trying to drag old Matthew back from the grave to tell him where the family loot was. At least it put me in a good mood.

I was right about Sheila, though she did break off when I arrived and offer to cook dinner. Over the meal I told her about chubby Norman and his unearthly pursuits.

'So it wasn't him?' she said.

'John seems to think not.'

'Well, who the blazes was it? The Wainwrights were the only family we'd been in touch with.'

'If we're right,' I said, 'and this really began with the Briefcase Incident, then that happened before you'd even started tracking the families. You'd only just got the birth certificates.'

'You mean it could be anyone connected with any of the six families. But that's God knows how many people!'

'It's worse than that, isn't it? It could be someone who isn't obviously connected with any of the families.'

'How d'you mean?'

'Like the Bartons. You've only found out about them by accident, more or less, but suppose one of the Bartons knows of the Sutton/Wainwright connection and wants to keep something hidden?'

'This is crazy!' she said. 'I'm researching people who must have been dead for most of the twentieth century. What the blazes can I unearth that might bother somebody nowadays? I mean, look at Smythe — he thinks it's a great joke having an ancestor who was nearly hanged and got transported for life instead.'

'Not everybody has Smythe's robust sense of humour, Sheila. And it probably isn't about the convicts themselves — it's probably about something between then and now.'

'What sort of thing?'

'Oh, I don't know. Suicide, insanity, disgrace, scandal, bad blood, illegitimacy, murder, perversion — there are all sorts of things that people don't like to be known about their families. Some people will get upset if a branch of the family has married beneath their social level. Everybody's got skeletons in their closet.'

'Poms!' she snorted. 'This whole thing is utterly ridiculous!'

'And what about the Aussies who tell everyone they're descended from starving peasants transported for sheep-stealing, or brave Irish rebels, when they're actually descended from rapists and murderers?'

'Sometimes,' she said, 'I wish I'd never bought that damned penny.'

'You're not thinking of giving it up?'

'No, I'm not!' she snapped. 'I am going to finish it and publish it and I don't care if some sneaking psychopath who hates cats doesn't like it. I just don't like having to look over my shoulder all the time.'

The phone rang and she went off to answer it, returning with a thoughtful look on her face.

'Guess what!' she said. 'That was young Smythe.'

'What? The schoolboy — Simon?'

'No, his elder brother, Stephen.'

'What did he want?'

'Wants to tell us some dark family secret. Says there is something I ought to know that his father didn't tell me.'

'And has he told you now?'

'No, he's coming up from London tomorrow evening to tell me in person.'

Stephen Smythe arrived early the following evening. He was in his mid-thirties, slighter built than his father (who must have been mortified by his son's neck-length hair) and casually dressed. He was very nervous.

After trying to relax him with a drink we could only sit and wait for him to open up. He didn't seem to be about to do so very fast.

'Mr Smythe,' said Sheila, after the pause had begun to embarrass everybody, 'you said there was something that your father hadn't told us. Was it about old John Smythe who was transported?'

He shook his head. 'No,' he said. 'Not really. He'll have told you all about him. Dad thinks that's a great joke. He doesn't mind talking about him. That's what makes it so bad.'

He paused again, took a gulp of his drink and started afresh.

'Look, me and my father don't exactly see eye to eye. He thinks that the Smythe family has some kind of military destiny. To hear him talk, you'd think we'd been soldiers ever since Agincourt.'

'We gathered that,' I said. 'Three generations which happen to include two World Wars isn't really much evidence for the proposition.'

'No,' he said, 'but he's fixated on it. Wants Simon to go to Sandhurst and all that. Wanted me to go to Sandhurst, for that matter.'

'But you didn't,' commented Sheila.

'No, and when I told him what I wanted to

do, he threw me out. That was years ago but I still only go home when he's away.'

I settled lower in my chair. If Smythe had driven a hundred and fifty miles to pour out his heart about his rotten relationship with his father it was going to be a very dull evening.

He pulled a thick brown envelope out of his jacket pocket.

'Did he tell you about Great-Aunt Alice?' he asked.

We nodded.

'Well, of course, she was his great-aunt really, not mine, but when she lived with us we all called her 'great-aunt'. She was the youngest child of the Smythe that wasn't hanged, as father calls him. Well, I was very fond of her when I was a kid. She was the one who always encouraged me to draw and paint and took my side when my father went on at me. If she hadn't died and left me some money, I wouldn't have been able to study art.'

He paused again, looked at the envelope in his hands then started anew.

'A few years before she died, one Sunday, we were all sitting round watching telly. It was Remembrance Sunday and the service was required watching in our house. Well, Great-Aunt Alice used to get pretty weepy and nobody took much notice, but that year — I think it was the year after the Falklands War — she got really upset. She said she couldn't watch any more and she went off to her room.'

Sheila refilled his drink and he drank gratefully.

'She didn't come down to lunch and in the afternoon Mum sent me up with a tray for her. When I went to her room she was in bed, but she was awake and it was obvious that she had been crying a lot. Well, I must have been about sixteen, and you know how an adult crying really throws a teenager. I asked her if she was all right and was there anything I could do. She said to sit down, that it was time I knew something. She had these papers on the bed and she showed me.'

He opened the envelope and took out a photograph. It was a standard Great War, postcard-sized portrait of a young man in khaki — a very young man.

'That's her brother,' he said, 'one of them — Great-Uncle Arthur.'

'He died in the Great War,' said Sheila.

'That's right. Dad was always telling us about John, the elder brother who'd fought in the Boer War and died in the Great War, and about my great-grandfather, James, who fought in the Great War and died just before I was born, but we never heard much about Arthur. All we knew was that he died in 1916. Well, I'd read the history books and I knew what a mess that war was, so I just thought that he'd gone 'Missing Presumed Dead' and no one really knew the details.'

'And hadn't he?' Sheila said. 'In 1916 there were a lot of places he could have died on the battlefield. Lots of blokes disappeared for ever.'

He shook his head again. 'No,' he said. 'He was at a base camp, a place called Etaples.'

'Where the big mutiny was,' commented Sheila.

'You know about the mutiny?'

'I'm a historian and I'm Australian,' she said. 'It was Aussies and Scots that started it, because a military policeman had shot a Scotsman over a girl.'

'That's right,' he said. 'He was there before the mutiny. He wrote his sister some letters.' He fumbled in the envelope and pulled out a worn letter, handing it to Sheila. 'Great-Aunt Alice left them to me. Here's one.'

She took the document, scanned it and read it aloud:

' 'Dear Sis, Thank you for your parcel. The food was very welcome I can tell you. The food here is awful. They get us up at five in

76

the morning and drill us and we don't get anything to eat till seven. Then we get one biscuit like a dog-biscuit. They call them double baked but they're so hard they must have been baked more than twice. We drill all day whatever the weather in a place called the bullring. When it is sunny it is like a desert and when it rains the sand is like a swamp and you can't march or drill properly. The drill instructors are absolute beasts, I can't tell you the things they do to people who make mistakes. We hate them because most of them have never been up the line and been shot at and all they do is shout at us and carry on all day. We cannot get any food except what we can buy at dinner time. There's a canteen run by some society ladies who sell tea and buns but apart from that we have to wait till evening. I can't wait to get out of here and go back up the line, but they won't let me go because they say I'm too young. I wasn't too young to join when I was fourteen but now there's been a fuss about underage boys in the trenches so we're all at Etaples until we're old enough to be sent back. I've been wounded twice but that was nothing compared to here. There's other things here that really make me sick. I can't wait to get home and see you all again. Your loving brother, Arthur. PS We call this place

Eat Apples and my friend Jimmy says that's because you would eat horse apples here.' '

She frowned slightly. 'What are 'horse apples'?' she asked.

'Horse manure,' I said. 'He certainly didn't pass that through the military censors.'

Sheila folded the letter and handed it back. 'Was he in the mutiny?' she asked.

'No,' he said. 'He got home on leave after that letter and he told his sister all about it, about the beatings by the drill instructors and everything. He told her that he was going crazy because they'd selected him as a marksman to be part of a squad that executed people — shot them to death. He said it was driving him mad. She said he cried like a baby when he told her.'

'And what happened?' I asked, though I thought I knew the answer.

He took another paper out of the envelope and handed it to Sheila.

'He never went back from his leave,' he said. 'He deserted.'

Sheila read the second paper:

' 'Number 863423 Smythe A. W. Private, First Battalion Wiltshire Light Infantry. On 24th June 1916 Private Smythe was granted seven days' leave from Etaples to return to England. After twenty-eight days he did not return to his unit and was accordingly posted as a deserter. Notification was sent to the military police and, by instruction of the Army Provost Marshal, officers called at his home but found him absent. Enquiries in the vicinity led to his arrest and interrogation, after which he was returned to his regiment at Etaples and detained in custody. On 6th August 1916 he was tried by court martial, found guilty and sentenced to death by firing squad. Sentence was duly carried out on the morning of August 13th.' '

Smythe was staring at the wall and his eyes were wet. 'That's what happened to Great-Uncle Arthur in the Great War,' he said bitterly, 'and poor old Alice wept for him all her life.'

'There was a war on,' I said quietly. 'Tough things get done in wartime.'

'Yes,' he said, 'and he'd done some of them, hadn't he. He'd volunteered under age. He'd been in the trenches, he'd stopped two bullets, and never complained. Then they left him at Etaples, bullied him and harassed him and turned him into an executioner, shooting his own mates at sixteen.'

He poured himself a long drink and swallowed it at a gulp. 'That's why there's no pictures of Arthur on Father's study wall. He can joke about old John who was nearly hanged, but he can't forgive a teenager who broke under the strain and was shot like an animal for it.'

'You want me to write about this?' asked Sheila.

'It's up to you,' he said. 'You can write about it or not. I just thought you ought to know about it. My sister rang to say that you'd been at Greyhanger. She was pretty fed up with the way Dad had gone on at you and she thought you were reasonable people. So I decided to tell you.'

He was calmer now that he'd said it all, maybe for the first time he'd ever mentioned it outside the family.

'Tell me,' I said, 'how strong is your father's devotion to his idea of a military dynasty of Smythes?'

'Absolute,' he said, promptly. 'He wants Smythes in the history books. That's why he was so co-operative with you and why he won't have a word whispered about poor Arthur.'

I told him about the threats against Sheila. He shook his head slowly.

'I suppose he might do that,' he said, 'but it doesn't seem like his sort of thing. He's always talking about action, always blathering on about suing the neighbours, or pulling their fences down or selling their ponies for wandering on our land, but he never actually does anything. He just freezes them in public. I can't really see him coming up here and killing your cat, although he doesn't like them. No, that's not his style at all. If he went after you, I'd have thought it would be merely a letter to *The Times*. Unless he's barmier than I thought, in which case I'd have thought he'd try something military, like a bomb.'

With which we had to be satisfied, but of course we weren't.

After Smythe had gone, Sheila asked, 'Do you really think it might be Smythe?'

'I don't know,' I said. 'We have to take account of his son's views, but he may not be the best person to make a dispassionate analysis.'

'Well, you did warn me about crazies who'd been trained to kill with a spoon. I suppose I'd just better keep clear of teacups and boiled eggs.'

9

The 'fan mail' kept coming, along with occasional telephone calls from newspapers who had picked up the story of Sheila's search from other papers. Occasional radio phone-in spots produced long lists of phone numbers to be checked out on the slender chance that the caller really did have some connection with the six convicts. Some of the mail was bizarre and some of it obscene after photographs of Sheila appeared in a couple of magazines. After the office mail-bag full of real problems every day, it was light relief to help Sheila sort her post in the evenings.

'I'm going to open a new file,' she remarked as we sat ploughing through the letters one evening. 'I'm going to call it 'Freckles'. Listen to this — 'Dear Sheila, I saw your picture in the magazine at my supermarket and I just love your freckles. Where did you get them?' It sounds as if he wants to buy some!'

'Where did you get them?' I asked. 'I read somewhere that freckles are a left-over from the Anglo-Saxon invasion, or the Vikings, or both, like red hair and Bure's Disease.'

'What's Bure's Disease?'

'It's a horrible disease that the Vikings left behind them when they came raping and pillaging up the River Bure. It still crops up in the villages in that area.'

'What about this,' she said, picking up another letter. ' 'Dear Miss McKenna, I am still at school, but I am very interested in history and when I saw your picture in the papers and read about your interesting research I wondered if there was any way that I could help you.' It's a posh school, too,' and she showed me the headed notepaper.

'Oh, very posh,' I said. 'Just the partner for a well-brought-up young lady, product of a sound religious education in Adelaide.'

'He just wants to help,' she said.

'He,' I said, 'lives for nine months of the year in a communal dormitory with a dozen other sweaty little sex-maniacs, whose greatest desire is to be let out so that they can outclass the Vikings.'

'You're a cynic,' she complained.

She read a couple more letters, then laughed. 'We really are pulling a better class of punter today. Look at this.'

The letter was on cream paper, headed with the green portcullis logo of the House of Commons, and had been passed on by the BBC in Birmingham. It said:

83

Dear Dr McKenna,

I happened to hear you on Carl Chinn's programme on Radio WM while in the West Midlands, telling the interesting story of your research. I am virtually certain that I can help you with the history of the man called Somers, who was one of my forebears. I live at Wilstock in the Cotswolds, and if you wish to make arrangements with my secretary I would be pleased to meet you and show the material I have on the dark secrets of my family.

Yours sincerely . . .

I laughed out loud at the signature.

'What's funny?' she demanded.

'He's a nutter,' I said. 'John Garton, MP, as he signs himself, is better known to the tabloids as 'Mad Jack'.'

'What does he specialise in?'

'He's a right-wing loony of some kind. Very vocal on race and immigration, champion of the rights of the 'common man' but vigorously anti-trade unions, thinks strikers should be jailed and homosexuals put in training camps, wants social security benefits cut, hates the European Union, detests the Euro, thinks the Scottish Parliament and the Welsh Assembly are nests of traitors who will cause the break-up of the Kingdom, loves the

Royal Family but feels free to comment loudly and often on their morals, and has a huge and solid majority in an East Midlands constituency.'

'Sounds fun,' she said, 'but at least he seems to be up front about the skeletons in his closet. So he doesn't sound like the kind of loony who murdered poor Buggalugs.'

'Who knows what kind of loonies you get in the House of Commons,' I said. 'Apart from plain old English corruption for money, we've had a member who lost his seat through a penchant for caning young lads, one round here who pretended he'd been eaten by sharks and ran off to Australia — he must have been barmy — a guy who got involved in a mysterious happening on Clapham Common, a bloke with a taste for soldiers, all the way back to a War Minister who slept with a girl who shared his favours with the Russian Defence Attaché.'

'Exactly,' she said. 'A representative cross-section of the British public. Isn't that what they're supposed to be?'

'They're supposed to be elected because they're smarter and better than the rest of us.'

'Huh!' she said. 'I shall phone his secretary tomorrow, and if you want to come with me you'd better be on your best behaviour.'

'Oh, I'm coming with you,' I said. 'I'm not having you disappear into some Cotswold dungeon to become the plaything of a foaming nutter dressed in skin-tight pink rubber with swastikas, who whips you three times before breakfast.'

'You make it sound real fun,' she said. 'I know it's a long time since breakfast and you can leave out the swastikas, but how about trying the rest of it?'

Which meant it was late morning before she phoned Garton's secretary but arrangements were duly made to visit Wilstock on the following Saturday.

* * *

Garton had sent his son, an amiable round-faced twenty-five-year-old, to meet us at the station and drive us to Wilstock. Perhaps because of being a social historian Sheila has a strong tourist strain, and as the car wove deeper into the Cotswolds she was breathless at the countryside and the little villages through which we passed.

'Wait till you see Wilstock, Dr McKenna,' young Garton told us, and he was right.

Wilstock, when we reached it, was a village green with a pool surrounded by ancient cottages and backed by an ancient church.

86

Our driver slowed as we passed through the centre.

'Wow!' Sheila said. 'I really didn't believe there was anything like this left in England. We thought you'd torn it all down to build airports and supermarkets.'

'Not with Dad around we won't,' said young Garton. 'He's a great believer in preserving England's green and pleasant land. That's why he lives here. It's inconvenient for his political work but he says he's got to keep an eye on it.'

We passed through the village and into a narrow lane that wound a couple of times before we stopped before a pair of wrought iron gates on stone pillars. Our driver pressed a button on the dash and the gates swung silently open.

'Dracula's castle stuff!' Sheila commented.

'Infra-red security,' Garton said. 'During the day they're on automatic for cars with the button. Anyone else has to use the gate phone to call the house. At night they're locked.'

'Your father values his privacy,' I said.

'It's not so much that, but he does seem to have a knack for upsetting nutters. Almost every time he appears on the telly we get shoals of mail and some of it is really nasty. He laughs about it, but it wouldn't be sensible to ignore the possibilities, would it?'

'I sympathise with him,' said Sheila.

'You've had that kind of experience?'

'Let's say if I'd known the response that my photos in newspapers would produce, I might have gone about my research a bit more discreetly.'

We had passed through the gates and come to a halt. On one side an array of flower beds flanked us, but on the left was a low, old, stone house — one of those easy, rambling houses that seem to have lain down to rest in a corner of English countryside and decided to stay there for three hundred years or so. I noted the leaded windows were the genuine article and thought how jealous Mrs Wainwright would be.

David Garton showed us in and as we looked around us at the low, timbered hall with its flagged floor, a door opened and a voice called from behind it.

'David! Take Dr McKenna and Mr Tyroll out the back and pour some drinks into them. I'll be with you in two shakes.'

In a couple of minutes we were sitting on the lawn at the rear of the house, under a cedar tree that seemed as old as the house, sipping our drinks. A door banged across the lawn and our host strode towards us. There was no mistaking the short, square figure, with bright, dark eyes and thick curls, still black despite his age.

'Dr McKenna!' he hailed her. 'How nice to see you. I'm so glad that my schedule permitted us to get together so quickly. Usually constituency business and the House mean that anything I want to do has to be delayed or cancelled.'

Having shaken Sheila warmly by the hand he turned to me. 'And Mr Tyroll — the redoubtable champion of the allegedly downtrodden in the West Midlands,' he said as he took my hand.

'I'm honoured that you know the name,' I said, only slightly sarcastically and more surprised actually.

'It's a politician's business to know everything about everyone,' he said. 'Or at least, to give the impression he does. You forget that there's more of your profession at Westminster than any other and they gossip like old women. When Dr McKenna told me who she was bringing along, I just dropped your name to a few Labour colleagues. They told me how much of a nuisance you were, so I thought you couldn't be so bad.'

We all grinned and he sat down. 'David,' he told his son, 'be a good chap and find out how long lunch is going to be while Dr McKenna and I share the dark secrets of your ancestry.'

As the young man walked away across the lawn, Garton explained. 'Wife's away in the States, so I'm dependent on the staff and on David to keep them in order. Now then, Dr McKenna, what have you got on my ancestor Jerry Somers?'

'First,' she said, 'it's Sheila for preference. Secondly, I've got his convict file,' and she delved into her bag for it.

'In that case, I'm Jack,' said Garton. 'I always thought Australia had it right about Christian names. And are you Chris or Christopher?' he asked me.

'Oh, definitely Chris — entirely egalitarian, me.'

Sheila shot me a glance of warning that said quite plainly, 'Don't be funny!' and laid her copy of the Somers file on the table.

Garton bent over it and pulled a pair of horn-rimmed glasses from his shirt pocket. 'Do you know,' he said, 'when I looked into the family past it never occurred to me that old Jerry Somers' file would still exist.'

'It doesn't occur to a lot of people,' said Sheila. 'But nearly all of the convict files are still available.'

He turned back to the papers, reading them out loud:

GERRY SOMERS No 48781
tried 18th June 1865,
arrived Fremantle Barracks March 1866.
Born 19th October 1840

Trade: Clerk   Height: 5 ft. 8 in.
Complexn: Dark   Head: Large
Hair: Black   Whiskers: Sides
Visage: Round   Forehead: High
Eyebrows: Black   Eyes: Black
Nose: Broad   Mouth: Wide
Chin: Rounded   Remarks: Well-spoken
Convict 7 years' transportation
Tried at Oxford, transported for riotous
   assembly
Character: Bad

He laughed when he reached the end. 'Well', he said, 'it's not a very flattering description, but I dare say it's accurate enough. In fact it might have fitted me when I was his age. The trade isn't quite right — he wasn't a clerk in the ordinary sense. He was a curate.'

'A curate!' Sheila exclaimed. 'You do mean a clergyman?'

'Oh, yes, indeed. Gerald Somers was a curate. But they got the description of his conduct right. They would have thought him very bad.'

'But if he was an educated clergyman, they probably put him down as a clerk because that was what they intended to use him as,' said Sheila. 'I noticed when I read his file that he'd got a long punishment record, and I couldn't understand it for a clerk. They usually got the soft options and were well treated but he wasn't.'

Garton shook his head. 'No. He certainly wasn't,' he said. 'Look at this — 'misbehaviour in church', 'refusal to obey an officer', 'unmannerly conduct', 'singing in cells', 'seditious conversation', 'treasonable songs' — what were 'treasonable songs', Sheila?'

'Anything the authorities didn't like — ballads about bush-rangers, Irish freedom songs, convict songs generally perhaps.'

Garton went on. ' 'Refusal to work' . . . '

I couldn't resist it. 'A striker?' I said.

'Yes,' said Garton quickly, 'and they gave him twenty-five lashes for it.' Sheila shot me an 'I warned you' smirk.

'It goes on and on, doesn't it?'

'Yes,' said Sheila. 'He was in trouble almost every month he was there. He served his full seven years and more as a prisoner and when he was released into the Colony his movements were restricted. He seems to have been quite a handful for a young clergyman.'

Garton grinned. 'Oh, he was,' he said. 'From anything I've ever learnt about him, he was.'

David came back and announced lunch in fifteen minutes.

'No hurry,' Garton told us. 'We'll take it out here if you don't mind. It's a beautiful day, far too hot to eat indoors.'

Over a lunch of cold meats and an excellent salad, Garton began to tell us about his unlucky ancestor.

'Jerrold Albert Somers, to give him his full name, was the fourth son of a family who'd been around here for generations. There's umpteen of us buried in the church up the road and one of us built this house. He wasn't terribly respectable, either. Edward Somers was a shipmaster, a privateer if you were polite — more truthfully a pirate. He built this house out of the profits of getting away with it, where Kidd and Co ended up at Execution Dock.'

'Where did he operate?' Sheila asked.

'Just about anywhere, I gather — the Pacific, the Indian Ocean, the Atlantic. Old Edward didn't mind so long as there were trading routes to keep him busy. Then when he'd built up a suitable retirement fund, he came home to England, sold his ships, bought some land, built himself a house, took a wife and set about being a country squire.'

'You sound like you admire him,' Sheila said.

'Well, I do. At least he did something a bit interesting. Old Edward and young Jerry are about the only two interesting ancestors I've got, and Jerry wasn't really my ancestor.'

'I thought he couldn't really be a direct ancestor, unless he came home,' said Sheila.

Garton shook his head. 'No,' he said. 'He never came home, so far as I know, and if he had he wouldn't have been acknowledged by the family. After Edward we settled down to being landed gentry, magistrates and so on. You can look that lot up in Burke's Landed Gentry, Somerses and Gartons. Jerry shook the family after generations of being dull and worthy.'

'I thought you approved of traditional English country life,' I said. 'Your son was telling us on the way how keen you are to protect the countryside.'

'I am,' he said, 'I am, but I don't want to turn it into a museum any more than I want the people in it to be stuffed dummies. Never forget that the blokes who made Britain great were mostly countrymen — Drake and Sidney, Raleigh, Frobisher, Hawkins, all that lot. They had their country houses but it didn't stop them ranging the seas. The men who went with them — they lived in cottages and when they weren't at sea they raised sheep and cows. You said you thought I admired Jerry Somers, Sheila, and I do. I might not have agreed with him if we'd met, but he got up and tried to do something about what he believed. That's a considerable virtue, so far as I'm concerned.'

'What did he do?' I asked. 'There can't have been many clergymen nicked for riot in his day.'

He laughed. 'No', he said, 'I don't suppose there were. It'd be quite unremarkable nowadays, wouldn't it? You have to have a few clergy to have a good demonstration nowadays, don't you? Anti-roads, anti-airports, animal rights, immigration, strikes, there's always a couple of them, and if they do get arrested, they get bound over, probably. And that's all that Jerry Somers did, really.'

'Took part in a demo?' I said.

'That's right. Church of England clergy seemed to have three choices in his day — turn Catholic, turn Socialist or get on with their job.'

'There weren't any Socialists in his day,' Sheila interjected.

'See — they really were good old days,' he joked. 'No, you're right, but ever since the Chartists, twenty-five years before, there'd been clergymen who got involved with radical movements and Jerry, in his day, became one of them.'

He pointed across the garden. 'His dad got him a curacy at Lower Barton — you can see the church spire from here. Thought he'd be able to keep an eye on him, I suppose, but it didn't work. His boss, Reverend Fanshawe, left Somers in charge of the little church with the poor people, while he preached to the nobs at St James' in Great Barton. Well, times got hard in the cloth trade and Jerry's parishioners were mostly weavers and blanket-makers. He'd always been a bit of a lefty at Oxford. His father had to get him out of a scrape or two there and stop him being slung out of college on more than one occasion.'

He looked thoughtfully at the distant spire beyond the garden. 'I suppose he believed that he was doing the Lord's work,' he went on. 'First he wrote letters to the papers, trying to draw attention to the plight of the people on his patch. That didn't do a lot of good, they just didn't print them. He went about tapping up the local big-wigs, persuading them to put a few quid in the kitty. That did a bit better, some of them had a conscience, but it wasn't enough. At least, it wasn't enough for young Jerry. He decided on a bit of action.'

'What did he do?' asked Sheila.

'He held a march. Nothing at all nowadays.

Every rag, tag and bobtail who thinks he's got a grievance gets up a march and nobody turns a hair, but back then people were easily frightened. Anyone over thirty could recall the Chartists, how they burned Stoke-on-Trent and seized a town up your way and held it for a fortnight, and they weren't having that in Oxford.'

'He marched in Oxford?' I said.

'He did, him and all his parishioners. He led the march and he made a speech. Well, if it had just been him and his flock there mightn't have been so much trouble, but he'd got some of his old pals at the university involved and a load of students joined in and things got out of hand. The city called the militia in to clear the streets and the police nicked everyone they could catch — that was Jerry and a few of his mob. The students had vanished.'

He broke off. 'David,' he said to his son, 'pop across to my study, will you, and bring me the box file marked 'Rev. Somers'?'

'All good stuff for your book, eh?' he asked Sheila while his son was away.

'Fascinating,' she said, 'if you don't mind me using it.'

He roared with laughter. 'After what the press has called me over the years there's nothing you could say that could come near it. Do you know, I was a hero when the Falklands row started, because I wanted to send an expedition and chuck them out? Then it was 'plain-spoken patriot Jack Garton'. Then a few weeks later I spoke on immigration and all of a sudden I'm 'right-wing extremist Jack Garton'. If you believed everything you read about me in the papers you'd have expected I had babies for lunch. You write what you see, Sheila, that'll do me. I might not like your opinions, but I'll buy a copy and stick it in the family archives.'

David arrived with the box file and his father opened it and extracted a bundle of typescript.

'That's the trial,' he said. 'I did track that down and have it typed up. Not that there's much in it. Just evidence of respectable citizens that they were present when the Reverend Jerry made a speech calling on the rich to pay attention to the needs of the poor.'

He thumbed through the pages. 'Here it is,' he said, and read, ' 'If the society in which we live cannot arrange for those who do its necessary work to have sufficient for their needs — sufficient to support themselves and their families and to lay a little aside against hard times — then it is high time that we changed the ways of our society and brought in one that cares for all.' '

'Not exactly revolutionary,' commented Sheila. 'And how did the witness manage to recall so exactly what Somers said?'

'Ah, well,' said Garton, 'that witness just happened to be a Justice of the Peace who just happened to have pocket-book and pencil at the ready. So he said. After that inflammatory speech, the students got out of hand, a few windows were broken, the Riot Act was read and the militia went in. End of riot.'

'And he got seven years' transportation for that,' I said. 'Why, he was an early harbinger of the Welfare State.'

'If you think I'm going to jump on that,' he said, 'you're wrong. I've got nothing against the Welfare State, so long as it gets its priorities right and looks after our people first and weeds out the layabouts. Still, you weren't looking for a speech, were you? I charge for them out of the House. Here's something that'll really interest you.'

He dipped into the box file again and produced a bundle of letters tied with old white tape.

'Those,' he said, 'are something you won't have expected to find — those are Jerry Somers' letters home to his family. How about that?'

Sheila's eyes were wide. 'Really?' she

gasped. 'That's wonderful. So few of them wrote. Even by the end of transportation only a third of English people could write, so there are very few letters.'

He handed them across the table. 'Unfortunately the correspondence was one-sided and it dried up. His father couldn't forgive him for bringing the family into disgrace and he wouldn't answer him, nor apparently let anyone else. You can read it in there, his entreaties for an answer, but he never got one and in the end he gave up.'

As Sheila delved into the letters, Garton turned to me. 'Well,' he said, 'Chris, you've heard all my dark secrets. What are yours? What was your father?'

'A fire-eater,' I said.

He laughed. 'I should have known. Well, you certainly took after him in your own way. Was he someone I should have heard about?'

'I doubt it,' I said. 'He performed under the title of 'Captain Flambeau'. He juggled and swallowed swords as well.'

'And your mother?'

'She was Welsh — a musician. She met my father on the Fringe at the Edinburgh Festival in 1963 and forgot all her chapel upbringing and went after him.'

'So you've got sawdust and music in the blood and you ended up a lawyer. What did your chapel-reared mum think about that?'

'She once told me that Adolf Hitler said that by the time he was done any German would be ashamed to be a lawyer. I always thought that Adolf was a pretty nasty character, so if he was against lawyers it seemed like a good thing to be.'

'He used them though,' said Garton.

'So he did — the kind that let him. I don't fancy being that kind.'

'Good for you,' he said. 'Good for you.'

He puffed at his pipe for a few moments. 'You know,' he said, 'we're not all that different. You stand up in court and say what must be said for your client — whoever he is. I stand up at Westminster and say what has to be said for my conscience — whatever it is.'

⋆ ⋆ ⋆

Sheila sat on the train homeward bound, her eyes still gleaming at the folder of photo-copies that Garton had given her.

'Well,' she said, 'he may be a Fascist beast, but he's a charming beast. Even you were getting along nicely with him.'

'I was being polite for your sake,' I said.

'Being nice my foot!' she said. 'Don't think I didn't hear you sneak in Adolf Hitler's name to see if you could get a rise out of him. Didn't work, did it?'

'I wasn't exactly expecting him to leap up and start singing the 'Horst Wessel',' I said.

'Huh,' she said. 'He even told you how alike you are and you never said a word.'

'Because we're not the least bit alike.'

'Oh, I don't know. He's got a certain dark charm.'

'Thank you, very much. You realise that he was only deploying his tweedy charm so that you will write about him nicely and say what a good bloke he is?'

'Doesn't look like he's got a dungeon or a whip,' she said, sadly. 'But then, he doesn't look like a nutter who'd murder a cat.'

'Nobody looks like a criminal nutter,' I said, 'or they'd all be safely locked up.'

'Well, you can't suspect him, anyway.'

'Why not?'

'Because he's given us all the dirt,' she said, tapping the folder.

'You mean he's given you all the dirt he wants you to know. He's also given you some amazingly good stuff for the book so you want to believe him.'

'Cynic,' she said and went back to poring over the Reverend Jerry's letters.

Once again, the darkness of the house and

garden when we got back home made me search them both carefully. Once again, there was nothing to be found, and once again I startled the old man taking his fat little dog for its late evening drag.

10

Sunday morning was warm and still, so we breakfasted outside. After food I was trying to read the papers, but Sheila was lolling about in bare feet, tight white shorts and a skimpy top.

'I thought,' I said, 'that Aussies cover themselves in grease and clothing when the sun's out, to avoid skin cancer.'

She glanced upwards. 'That,' she said, 'is not what I would call sunshine. Anyway, it's nice to expose yourself without feeling guilty.'

'You might not feel guilty, but it's what I'm feeling that matters.'

She unwound herself from the sun-lounger. 'You poor old article! Once a morning too much for you, is it? Aren't you allowed to do it twice on Sundays?'

She raised a hand before I could respond. 'No! Don't worry, I shall take myself off and meditate beside the pool.'

She sauntered down the lawn towards the little pool at the bottom. The fine weather had set the solar fountain spurting enthusiastically, which didn't do me any good either.

Half-way to the pool she called out, 'My

oath! Who cut the cheese?'

'What's wrong?'

'Your pool stinks,' she said.

I got up and walked down to join her at the poolside. She was right. The warm air was ripe with something quite nasty and the cause wasn't far to seek. A dead pigeon floated in the middle of the pool surrounded by a thin rainbow-coloured scum.

'How did that get there?' I wondered aloud.

'Who cares?' she said. 'Perhaps it was flying over and dropped dead. Maybe it felt like a dip because it was hot yesterday and got drowned. The problem is getting the darned thing out.'

I could see what she meant. The solar spray's circulation of the water was pushing the bird's corpse up against the fountain's base in the centre of the pool, from which it couldn't be reached from the shore.

'I can turn the fountain off,' I said, and opening the little control box on the pool's rim I did so. It made no difference at all.

'I think it's caught in the fountain,' she said.

'The pool's not deep. Wade in and yank it out,' I suggested.

'Yair! And get Pommy pigeon's toe-rot? No, thank you. Have you got a pair of gumbos — wellies?'

'There's a pair just inside the shed door. They're mine, so they ought to fit you.'

She scowled and ambled off to the little shed at the bottom of the garden, returning in a couple of minutes with the boots and a pair of gardening gloves. I was making ineffective attempts to swat the dead bird away from the fountain with a rolled-up newspaper.

'You daft galah!' she said. 'You'll fall in. Leave it to an expert.'

She sat on the little stone bench by the pool and pulled on one of the boots. As she pulled on the second boot she gasped, then gave vent to a long, rising cry.

'Oh, my God! Get it off me!'

I spun around to see her sprawled back on the bench, her fists clenched at her sides, both legs working in the air like pistons.

'Get it off me, Chris! Get it off me!' she wailed.

I snatched at one of her wellingtons and tugged at it, but she booted me away, gasping, 'The other one! The other one! Get it off me, for God's sake!'

She was as white as a sheet, her freckles standing out like a spray of blood and her breath heaving between her desperate cries.

I grabbed her right boot, managed to get a grip despite her writhing, and tore it off. As soon as it was off, Sheila collapsed on to the bench in a huddle, rolled up tightly.

'Can you walk?' I asked.

She shook her head. 'Not in bare feet,' she whispered.

I scooped her up and carried her into the house, leaving her on a couch while I found the brandy and poured us both a large one. I pressed the glass into Sheila's hand and she uncoiled and gulped it down gratefully. As she drank I examined her foot carefully but found no marks of anything.

'What on earth was it?' I asked.

She shuddered. 'Don't ask!' she said. 'Something moved in the toe of the boot as I pulled it on. Something wriggled! Go and look!'

I left her with another brandy and went back into the garden. Picking up the right boot I shook it upside down. A thin plastic bag dropped out, inside which were the partly squashed remains of a spider — far larger than any British variety I had ever seen. I shook the boot again, then nerved myself and slid my hand into it. A piece of card was stuck in the ankle part. I pulled it out and read the message on it:

NOSY MISS MUFFET
SAT OF A TUFFET
TO PULL ON HER WELLIES, 'TIS SAID.
A GREAT HAIRY SPIDER
WAS LURKING INSIDE HER
BOOTS, AND NOW NOSY IS DEAD.

Sheila was asleep on the couch when I went back indoors. I called John Parry and caught him off duty, so I invited him for a drink.

While I waited for him, I went back to the pool and examined the dead pigeon more carefully. It was an ordinary, common or garden wood pigeon, the kind that, I suppose, occasionally dies in awkward places, but it hadn't died in my pool. It had been put there and tied into position with a short length of fishing line tied to a stone. I left the evidence in place for John.

When he arrived I gave him the latest details. Together we looked at the trap that had been set in the pool, then I cremated the pigeon on the rubbish heap.

Sheila was dozing in the sitting-room, so we settled into the kitchen with a couple of beers.

'You've still no idea who's doing this?' he asked.

I shook my head. 'According to you it wasn't Norman Wainwright who killed

Buggalugs. I can't see it being Jack Garton, but I can't really see it being Captain Smythe, either.'

'I can check Smythe out,' he said, 'the same way I checked Wainwright.'

'Would you?' I said. 'I'd be grateful.'

'There's not much more I can do,' he said. 'The Chief Constable would not be terribly amused if he found me spending precious time and money on a spider in somebody's welly, bach.'

'Not just a spider,' I said, picking up the plastic bag. 'That bloody thing! Look at it!'

'I think they call them bird-eating spiders,' he said. 'There's a number of shops that sell them. They're tropical and they can give you a nasty bite, I believe.'

'It wasn't going to bite,' I said. 'He didn't want it to bite. It was there inside that bag so that it would be felt when someone pushed their foot in. That was enough.'

'I never thought Sheila would be scared of spiders,' he said. 'Did you know that?'

'No,' I said, 'and that makes it more puzzling and worrying. Who the blazes does know that and how do they know?'

He frowned thoughtfully. 'The first episode — the cat. I always thought it was someone close to you — geographically, I mean.'

'But surely, he came here to deliver his

nasty little threat and came across Buggalugs by chance, didn't he?'

'No he didn't,' he said. 'He brought with him two laser-printed notes that referred to cats, prepared in advance. If it really was Norman or the gallant Captain, then they must have known you had a part-time moggy. Now it's worse, because he knows something about Sheila that you didn't.'

I nodded. 'I can't understand how he knew that Sheila would pull the boot on. They're mine.'

'Doesn't matter, does it?' he said. 'If you had pulled them on, what would you have done?'

'I'd have made a face when I felt the thing squash and pulled off the boot and shaken it out.'

'Right, boyo, and Sheila would still have seen a dirty great squashed spider and the card and known it was for her. She'd have thought about what it would have been like if she'd put the boot on and I dare say that would have been worse for her than what actually happened.'

Not long afterwards Sheila joined us. She had showered and her hair was still wet and she was wrapped in a dressing-gown of mine, but she had recovered most of her colour and was even smiling slightly.

'Hello, possums!' she said nervously. 'Isn't it nice that when I get fatally bitten by a giant spider, he calls his mate in and settles down for a gargle.'

'Not at all, cariad,' John said. 'His first thought was to send for the forces of law and order to protect you. You knew it was a spider?'

She screwed up her face. 'I thought it was a spider. It moved like a spider. Was it?'

'Yes, it was,' he said, and showed her the plastic bag and the card.

'So, it's our friendly maniac again,' she said, making a grimace.

'Who knew you didn't like spiders, Sheila?' John asked.

'Nobody here,' she said. 'You feel such a drongo, being frightened of spiders — particularly here, where you haven't even got any poisonous ones.'

'I'm scared of heights,' John volunteered. 'Put me two stairs up and I'm helpless.'

She took a beer from the fridge and sat down with us, staring at the card and the bag.

'It started when I was a kid. I don't know why. We used to frighten each other at school about getting bitten on the bum by spiders in the dunny. When the school toilets were being replumbed and they put a temporary arrangement outside, I almost bust my plumbing staying out of it till I could get home. It's just not something I mention to people, you know. It makes you feel such a galah.'

'So nobody in England knew about it?' John persisted.

She shook her head. 'Not even Chris,' she said.

'Somebody did, though, didn't they?'

11

Later in the day John ventured on dangerous ground.

'I suppose,' he said, 'that your research is nowhere near finished, Sheila?'

'No,' she said. 'I've done the easy bit so far. I've found three families who weren't very difficult because they know who they are and where they come from. I haven't had a flicker on the other three. They might have died out, of course, but it's more likely that they simply haven't caught on to any connection because they don't know much about their ancestry. If their names have changed since the 1860s, they wouldn't necessarily make the connection.'

'So what do you do next?'

'I start trudging through birth certificates in the Family Records Centre and census returns.'

'Where are they?'

'They're in the County Records Offices but they're also on the Internet up to 1891.'

'So you won't have to travel to consult them?'

'Well, it's not just the census returns. These

blokes shipped out in 1865 — right? I know where each of them was born from his birth certificate, and his parents' names. I locate them in the County Census and work forward, looking for their children through the census records, and as I go I try to cross-check and fill in family details from any other references I can find in the County archive.'

'How far does that take you?' asked.

'Down to 1891,' she said. 'The 1901 census hasn't been released yet.'

'And what do you do beyond 1891?' asked John.

'Well, so long as they haven't shifted about too much, it should be possible to pick them up again from gravestones, baptismal registers, electoral registers, street directories, trade directories, local newspapers, but it'll be pretty time-consuming.'

'And you'll still have to do a bit of travelling, won't you?' John said.

'Yes,' she said. 'And I'm afraid I'm just going to have to do it. Funnily enough, I don't feel so worried about that after this morning. He's pinched my briefcase on the way from London and duffed my car in Somerset, but his really nasty efforts have both been here. I don't think he'd actually attack me away from home.'

'You can't tell,' I said. 'He (or she) is obviously unbalanced.'

'Yes, but so far he (or she) has only threatened — not attacked.'

'That could end at any moment,' said John. 'Since you don't know what it is that he thinks he's protecting, you won't know if you stumble across it and that might trigger him off. If all his attempts to stop you finding it fail, then he may simply try to stop you publishing.'

'I suppose that's right,' she said, 'but I intend to finish my research and write my book, so don't try and persuade me not to.'

John backed off. 'All right, all right,' he said. 'I know better than that. But you want to think about how you do things.'

'Like how?'

'Don't travel by car — '

She interrupted with a laugh. 'I haven't got one, remember. Somebody swiped it and your wonderful English police have so far failed to find it!'

'I know, I know, but just be careful, take the train, keep your eye on people around you when you're working. See who's using the same files, keep your eyes peeled for someone who could be watching you. Oh yes, one more thing — shake your boots out before you put them on.'

'Right,' she said. 'You go on looking for my car and I'll get on with the job.'

So she did. I wasn't at all happy about it, but for the next few weeks she was here, there and everywhere. Down to London, off to Staffordshire, Shropshire, Warwickshire, Birmingham. I was uneasy all the time. Every day I was nervous until I knew she was home. Every time we went out together — to the pictures, to restaurants or whatever — I searched the house and garden.

Nothing happened.

Sheila got bored with the remorseless hard slog of tracking the remaining three families and would occasionally go back on aspects of the first three. She asked me to write to the Bank of England about Uncle Matthew Wainwright's fabled gold. I did and had a reply from the Secretary to the Bank:

Dear Mr Tyroll,

It is usually a surprise to the general public to be told that there are, in fact, very few unclaimed deposits in the Bank's hands. I am sorry to tell you that there is no account here under any of the names you have suggested.

'You should send that to Mrs Wainwright and Norman,' Sheila said.

'Not likely! They wouldn't believe it. They'd want to know why I'd enquired, and it might fuel any belief that you really are Cousin Matilda from Oz come to scoop the loot.'

'I suppose so,' she said. 'Where can I find out about these pirates?'

'Pirates?'

'Yes. Jack Garton's ancestor sounds as if he might give me an interesting chapter, but there isn't much about him in the stuff Garton gave me.'

'Try Esquemeling's *History of the Buccaneers of America*.'

'Where would I find that?'

'In the study — somewhere behind the door. It's a battered old dark red book with silver titling.'

'Do many piracy cases, do you?'

'No. I told you, my mother had some weird books and I inherited them.'

Half an hour later she was back. 'Esquemeling,' she said, 'is very good on all the pirates you already know about, but I can't find anything about Edward Somers. Got any other ideas?'

'Try the Internet,' I said. 'Isn't the truth supposed to be out there. Bang in 'skull+crossbones' and see what comes up.'

That did the trick. An hour later she was

back with some sheets of printout.

'Sometimes,' she said, 'you have good ideas. Have a look at this.'

It was a graphic print of an eighteenth-century pamphlet called 'A narrative of the Exploits of Edwarde Somers the Privateer'. On the front was a crudely cut woodblock illustration of a bow-legged man in a wide-brimmed hat, armed with cutlass and pistol.

'Look at the last page,' she said.

I looked and saw quickly what she meant:

While the *Revenger* was being refitted in Bluefields Captain Somers took a wife, none other than a black wench from the Barbadoes who served the topers at the sign of the *Three Gallions*. When the *Revenger* weighed anchor the Captain's new wife was aboard her and, when Somers fell in with the Spaniard *Esmeralda* and took her, it was rumoured that Mrs Somers did as much execution upon the Spaniard's crew as any man of the *Revenger's* company and was voted a full share by the crew. Made rich beyond his dreams by the treasure taken from the *Esmeralda*, Somers then sailed for Bristol, where he, as was the custom of his calling who had the good fortune to leave their profession by their own choice, sold his *Revenger* to his mate, Robert Fortune and, as the sailors say, swallowed the anchor, for he purchased lands and built a fine house, determining never to go to sea again. Nor did he, but lived many years on his estate, where he was esteemed an amiable man, not above taking a pot at the alehouse with men of any station and where his handsome wife was pointed out for her custom of taking a pipe of tobacco with the men.

I laughed. 'So Mad Jack Garton has got West Indian blood! What a turn-up! I said he'd only told you the secrets he didn't mind you knowing.'

'Too right,' she said. 'Still, it's another interesting bit for the book. Where's Blue-fields?'

'On the Atlantic coast of Nicaragua. Real old pirate territory. The population is still a mix of European, Negro and local blood and the town itself is named after a Dutch pirate.'

'Sounds picturesque. I bet the Three Gallions was a dandy of a pub. I just love the idea of a black barmaid from there ending up as lady of the manor in that little Disney village we went to. Wonder if there's any pictures of Mrs Somers about anywhere. Let the world see the face that turned Edward Somers into a landed gentleman.'

'Have you thought about another aspect of this?' I asked.

'What's that?' she said. 'Don't tell me you're chicken about revealing the skeleton in Mad Jack's closet.'

'Not at all,' I said, 'but you should consider that it may also have given us another suspect.'

Suspects! Chubby Norman? Probably not. Captain Smythe? Possibly or possibly not. Now Mad Jack Garton. Possibly. And all the other three so-far-undiscovered families and everybody's sisters and cousins and aunts and uncles and children and nephews and God knows who.

12

The next day was spoiled before it had begun. A glance at my office diary revealed that Julian Sawney had an appointment to see me late in the day. The timing didn't really matter; an appointment with Sawney always spilled its gloom across the whole day.

He was his usual pompous, irritable self when he arrived.

'Mr Tyroll,' he said, 'I've already explained about that outrageous affair of the radio that was stolen in the boarding house where I live.'

'Yes, Mr Sawney,' I said.

'Well,' he said, 'just look at this!'

He drew a sheet of paper from his inside pocket and flung it onto my blotter. I didn't need to read it to see that it was a charge sheet. I read it:

Julian Nugent Sawney on or about the third day of April entered the premises of William Thomas as a trespasser and while therein stole a Kanya battery/mains stereo radio/cassette recorder property of the said William Thomas.

'Burglary,' I said.

'But I've told you — I didn't!'

'As a matter of fact,' I said, 'you told me that you hadn't suborned some fellow lodger to steal the radio. You didn't tell me that you hadn't burgled it yourself. You said that she was saying you persuaded her to steal it.'

'That's what she was saying then.'

'And what's she saying now?'

'That I stole it and gave it to her.'

'So, she's been charged with receiving the radio knowing it to have been stolen, yes?'

'No — she's a witness against me.'

'Unsupported evidence of an accomplice,' I reminded him. 'What other evidence have they got?'

He looked more untrustworthy than usual. 'They have a statement from me.'

'Saying what, precisely?'

'I don't know.'

'Mr Sawney, if you made the statement you must know what it says.'

'I was upset, Mr Tyroll — very upset. I really can't recall what I said.'

'Wonderful!' I said. 'Never mind. Where's the notice with the serial number of the interview? I can get a copy of the tape.'

'It isn't on tape.'

Police forces have been taping interviews for more than fifteen years. I couldn't remember when I last saw a written confession statement. As soon as scientific document examination began to prove that some paper statements were forgeries, they moved to tape-recording. It's far harder to prove any faking.

'Why is it on paper? Did you ask to make a written statement?'

'No. I didn't want to make a statement at all.'

'Mr Sawney, even under the latest rules they can't force you to make a statement. Did you ask them to call me or the duty solicitor?'

'Yes, but they said they couldn't get hold of you and I'd have to wait ages.'

I sighed. Anyone trying to decide whether Julian Sawney or the Central Midlands police are lying is wasting their time. I looked at the charge sheet.

'It says here that you were charged at 21.42 on the night before last.'

'Yes, about then.'

'I was at home. I was available.'

'Well, I didn't know that. I only know what they told me. They said they couldn't find you.'

'Why on earth you, of all people, should believe a policeman I do not know. Still, you made a written statement and you don't know what it says.'

'No,' he said.

'Who wrote it? You or them?'

'One of them did. I can't write very quickly.'

'But you signed it?'

'Yes.'

'And did they make you write the bit at the end which says, 'I have read the above statement and I have been told that I can add, alter or correct anything I wish'?'

'They made me copy something out that was on a card, printed in capitals.'

'That will have been it,' I confirmed. 'It's called the 'caption' and it makes it very difficult to say afterwards that you didn't mean what's in the statement. As you may find.'

'But I didn't read the statement!'

'Why not?'

'It was in the policeman's writing. I can't read handwriting.'

'Why not, Mr Sawney?'

'I have trouble. I was in a road accident. It caused a form of epilepsy. I can't read handwriting or small print.'

I looked at the folded racing paper in his pocket and said nothing.

'They read it out to me and then I signed it.'

'Why?'

He looked at me with astonishment — the first time he'd looked at me directly since he came in. 'I had to. There were two of them.'

'They frightened you?' I asked.

'Of course. I didn't know what they would do to me.'

'They have to put you before a magistrate in the morning,' I said. 'They don't like putting prisoners up who're covered in blood and bruises and plasters and bandages. It's bad for the image.'

'What are we going to do about it, Mr Tyroll?'

'At the moment we are going to do precisely nothing. When I get a copy of the mysterious statement you made and the summary of their case from the Crown Prosecution Service, then we can think about what to do.'

'But if I get convicted it'll trigger off the suspended sentence, won't it?'

'Certainly, but you should have thought of that before signing your name to a statement which you had neither written nor read.'

'They did read it over to me,' he said.

'You won't be terribly surprised, will you, when we get a copy of it and there are bits in it which they didn't read out, will you?'

'Might that happen?'

'It's been known,' I said.

'Sometimes,' he said, starting to get pompous again, 'I think that you are not very sympathetic to my problems, Mr Tyroll.'

'Mr Sawney,' I said, 'there's nothing in the rules that says I have to sympathise with you, only that I have to try and defend you to the best of my ability within the law. Good afternoon.'

At home I slumped into a chair and made vague motions for a large drink. Sheila brought me one.

'Bad day?' she asked.

'In capitals,' I said. 'Sawney was my last client of the day. Came into the office with a newspaper in his pocket, folded to the racing page, and sat and told me that he could only read capitals.'

'You think he was lying?'

'I always think Sawney is lying, and I'm usually right.'

'If you don't want to defend him, why do it?'

'Comes with the territory,' I said. 'It's the court's job — not mine, or the police, or the Crown Prosecution Service — to decide who's guilty. If I start treating clients as if I think they're guilty I might as well pack up.'

'But surely you can pick and choose?'

'As a matter of fact, under the Law Society

rules I can only refuse a client's instructions for good reason. The mere fact that I don't like him, that I don't trust him and that most of the time I think he's guilty, isn't a sufficient reason.'

'What about the crimes people are charged with? Can't you refuse to defend certain kinds of crimes?'

'Strictly speaking, no, though some firms won't defend rape charges or child molestation or animal cruelty. That's the worst reason in the world, though. Once you start picking and choosing who's going to have a defence you've voted for tyranny.'

'Gloom, gloom,' she said, and poured me another drink. 'Do you want to hear my good news?'

'Go on,' I said, 'lighten the terrible darkness of my soul.'

'Huh! Whoever said lawyers have souls? Anyway, look at this.'

'This' was a letter. The fan mail had been dwindling as the media attention dropped off, and much of what did arrive was repeat letters from nutters who'd already written a number of times. This seemed to be a new one. It was typed on unheaded cream bond from an address in Lancashire. It said:

Dear Dr McKenna,

I do not live in Staffordshire, but I still visit friends in that area. While there recently I saw a piece in the *Staffordshire Sentinel* about your search for the relatives of a man called Simmonds. I think you'll find that the family are now called Lewis, though they still live in Staffordshire. I have a certain amount of information that may help you and would be happy to meet you and discuss it. On the 14th I shall be in Staffordshire. Perhaps we could meet at the lounge bar of the Oak Tree Hotel in Moorstall about 8.30 p.m. I know it's a little out of your way, but it's the best I can suggest in the near future. Perhaps you would care to ring me at the number above and let me know if this will be convenient.

Yours sincerely, Alan Lewis

'So,' I said, 'a breakthrough in Staffordshire at last.'

'Yes, and it looks good. I'd already found out that the direct male line of Simmondses died out in the generation after my man and the descent is through a family called Lewis, so it looks like this guy's one of them and might save me a lot of slog.'

'And what are the Lewis family? Your researches seem to have been moving steadily

128

up the social scale. Mrs Wainwright, lower middle class; Captain Smythe, middle class; Mad Jack, upper middle class. I was really hoping to get an invite to Buckingham Palace when you finally discovered that the Royals are descended from one of your lot.'

'Can't be,' she said, 'or Oz wouldn't be trying to sack the Queen. If she was of good old convict stock they'd build her a palace in Sydney. Seriously, though, the reason why I got on to those first three is exactly because of class.'

'What do Aussies know about class? You're always telling the world yours is a classless society!'

'Yair,' she said. 'Drop round the Capital Territory pubs on a pay night and you're bound to find the Governor-General having a gargle with some of his ocker mates then slipping out the back for a spot of two-up. But that doesn't mean we don't know about class. We have social historians, very clever ones, who've studied it and know how the great British religion works.'

'If you're going to lecture me on social equality, I'm going to have a shower and you can cook dinner all alone,' I said.

'What I was about to say was that the working class in England don't have the same kind of interest in their ancestors that the middle class do. That's why I haven't been contacted by the other families, I expect. The first three moved up scale or stayed up, but the other three either stayed down or went down, so they're the ones that are hard to locate.'

Later in the evening she phoned Lewis. When she came off the phone she looked slightly puzzled.

'What's the problem?' I asked.

'Nothing really,' she said. 'We're meeting him at the Oak Tree on the 14th. It was just his accent — posh English.'

'What does he do for a living?'

'He said he's a salesman for an electronics company. He was on a mobile.'

'Whereabouts?'

'How do I know where he was? He could have been in Adelaide for all I know!'

'I meant did he say where he was?'

'No. There was music in the background.'

'Jukebox? Television? Band? Radio?'

'Well, it wasn't a jukebox, anyway. It was Grieg's Piano Concerto.'

'How very un-working class,' I said.

13

Moorstall is a tiny village in a fold below the Staffordshire moors, up near the Potteries. The Oak Tree Hotel is actually about two miles from the village, up a country road.

I had become tactically defensive in my thinking. As our cab pulled into the pub's forecourt I noted with approval a moderate number of expensive cars parked outside. It seemed an upmarket sort of establishment, not the sort of place where anyone was likely to try any malarkey.

The lounge bar, a large comfortable room with low lights, was quiet, with only a handful of blokes in business suits at the bar, all of whom seemed to know each other and each other's business. All of the tables were untenanted, so we took one which gave us a wide view of the bar and both its doors. It was about fifteen minutes until our contact was due.

The fifteen minutes passed, and another. I looked at my watch.

'Your man's late,' I remarked. 'Another drink?'

While I got the drinks I took the

opportunity to ask the bartender if he knew Lewis. He screwed up his eyes, thought for a moment, then said that he couldn't actually recall anyone of that name but he might know the face. I told him that Lewis was a salesman in the electronics line. He screwed up his face again and still couldn't recall him.

'The barman doesn't know our bloke,' I told Sheila.

'No reason why he should,' she said. 'He did say he was only round here occasionally.'

We gave him an hour, then I went to the bar and asked for a phone.

'Not got your mobile, sir? There's a payphone outside in the lobby, sir.'

I followed his pointing finger and found the phone. I called the mobile number that Lewis had given, but it was switched off. On the wall above the phone was a taxi firm's card. It had a mobile phone number, but lots of one-man firms do. I called it and asked for a car to Stafford.

We had just finished our drinks when the bar door opened and a bearded face wearing shades looked in. 'Anyone call a taxi?' it asked.

We followed the elderly driver out on to the car park. A few yards from the pub's door a red car stood, with 'Moorstall Taxis' in adhesive lettering across its rear window.

Something flickered in my mind, but it was the name I had seen on the card by the payphone.

As the driver slid into his seat I opened the rear door for Sheila. As she slid in, the driver reached through his open window and touched my arm. 'Did you drop something there, by the door, sir?'

He pointed towards the pub's door. I turned and saw something lying at the foot of the step. I moved across the car-park and had almost reached the doorway when my brain switched on. Suddenly I remembered that private hire cars are not allowed to carry the word 'taxi' anywhere on them — it's illegal.

In the same instant I heard a car door slam behind me and, as I spun around, the red car shot away across the car-park and out into the road, disappearing fast along the road towards the slope of the moor.

I plunged headlong through the pub's door and grabbed the payphone, dialling 999. While I gasped out the details to the police operator, the barman emerged into the lobby.

As I put the phone down he looked at me quizzically.

'Spot of bother, sir?'

'The taxi-driver who looked into the bar,' I said. 'Did you know him? Is he local?'

He shook his head. 'Didn't really see him,'

he said. 'Bearded bloke, wasn't he? Didn't look like anyone I've ever seen.'

I pointed to the card taped to the wall. 'Is that your local taxi firm?'

He peered at it. ' 'Moorstall Taxis'? No, sir. There's only one firm hereabouts, that's Colin's Cars in the next village. How did that get there?'

He moved to take the card down, but I stopped his hand.

'Leave it,' I said. 'The police will want to see that.'

'Police?' he queried. 'Has there been something wrong?'

The only thing that stopped me knocking the fool senseless on the spot was the sound of two police cars arriving outside. Seconds later a uniformed sergeant and three constables piled through the door.

As succinctly as I could I told my story to the sergeant. Luckily he was clear-headed and fast. Once he'd got the gist he went into action.

'If he went that way,' he said, 'he's got two choices. The road splits below the moor. One way'll take him towards Stoke, the other'll take him up on to the moor.'

He paused for a couple of seconds only. 'Evans,' he told one of his constables, 'cut round the bottom of the village and see if you can head him off on the Stoke road. Parsons, get on to the nick — all available cars to cover both options. Come on, sir. Come with me. We'll have a look at the moor road.'

'You think that's more likely?' I asked.

'If he doesn't want to attract attention to whatever he intends to do, yes,' he said, which didn't make me feel the least bit better.

★ ★ ★

As the fake hire car leapt away from the Oak Tree Sheila was flung heavily back in the rear seat. By the time she had righted herself the vehicle was barrelling along a dark country road at dangerously high speed, the bearded driver hunched over the wheel.

'What are you doing?' she said, trying to sound desperate, which she was, and helpless, which she never is.

The driver lifted his head slightly. He freed his left hand from the wheel and took a knife from the seat beside him, showing it to her briefly.

'You know what I'm doing, Dr McKenna. I'm taking you away to somewhere where we can discuss your researches in private and where I can leave you with a souvenir that will remind you not to interfere with me.'

'You're going to kill me!' she said, still

trying to sound terrified.

'Not,' he said, 'unless you make that unavoidable. If I'd wanted to kill you, I could have done it a dozen times by now.'

She started to sob, noisily.

'There's no need for you to be afraid,' he said. 'I've told you — I merely want you to understand that you must stop what you're doing. You haven't taken any notice of my previous warnings, so I shall have to inflict a very little pain, but that is only so that every time you look in a mirror you will remember that you must not go on with your pointless researches.'

She remembered that this must be the lunatic who had slit Buggalugs' throat and sabotaged the wellington boot and her anger almost made her risk trying to take him from behind, but he had the knife and the car was still travelling at high speed. If she tackled him now they might both get killed. Sooner or later he would have to stop to do his dirty work.

At a junction in the road he swung left, never slackening speed. Above the road on their left the ground climbed. It was now nearly full dark and Sheila was aware of a solid bulk of land looming above them. She fell to sobbing noisily again while she tested both of the rear doors and slipped the lock button off the nearside door.

After about three miles the driver slowed, wrenching the car into a tight turn between two weathered posts at the roadside and into an unmade track. Under cover of the vehicle's jolting along the track, Sheila sprawled along the rear seat, her head at the driver's end and her left hand grasping her shoulder-bag firmly.

A particularly heavy jolt slowed the car and distracted the driver. In a second she was up, ramming the bottom edge of her heavy bag into the back of his neck. As he lost his grip on the wheel, she activated her personal alarm and dropped it on the front floor. Her instincts were right — instead of reaching for the knife he scrabbled for the screaming device on the floor.

Sheila doubled over like a spring in the rear seat, wrenched open the nearside door and catapulted herself out, rolling into the undergrowth at the edge of the track.

Oblivious to scratches and bruises she sprang up and looked for the driver. The car had halted a few yards further up the track and he was climbing out. She ran as hard as she knew how, pounding back down the track towards the road, not knowing whether to expect a shot as she ran.

I was in the back of the sergeant's police

car, trying to keep my seat while the car racketed along the dark, narrow road, and I hunched forward so as not to miss anything passing on the radio.

As we came to the junction the constable driving asked, 'Left or right, sarge?'

'Left,' the sergeant snapped. 'They've seen nothing towards the town. Let's see if he's made for the moor.'

His words reminded me again that Sheila was in the hands of the madman who had left poor Buggalugs bleeding on my back doorstep. It was dark and the slope of the moor hung over us — moorland that went on and on, through the Peak into Yorkshire, and that was largely empty.

Our driver slowed suddenly.

'What're you doing?' the sergeant demanded.

'Look, sarge,' said the driver, and I leaned further forward.

The headlights had just picked up a figure coming around the next bend in the road. It was Sheila, jogging as easily as though she were out for a morning's exercise.

14

John Parry rang me at the office midway through the following morning.

'I have had,' he said, 'a bewildered inspector of the Staffordshire police on the blower.'

'What was bewildering him?' I asked.

'Well, he filled me in on your adventures of last night on his patch but he seemed to find it difficult to believe your account of how it all began.'

'I hope you put him straight?'

'Oh, definitely, boyo. I explained to him that, although superficially members of two respectable professions, you and your intended had a capacity for falling into troubles that nobody else knew existed.'

'Unfair!' I said. 'We are always innocent victims.'

'Victims you may well become if you continue on your melodramatic way, but innocent strikes me as an actionable misdescription, boyo.'

'I take it you didn't just ring up to abuse me and the woman that I love, John?'

'No, no,' he said. 'I rang up to tell you the

139

good news — kidnapping being a serious matter, prohibited by the Offences Against the Person Act, I can now take a more active part in this affair, for which reason I would like to come and see you both this evening, if convenient.'

'You mean you're after a free meal, Detective Inspector Parry?'

'Bribery, boyo — the life's-blood of the police service — as no one knows better than you. What can a man do when faced with temptation, except succumb to it?'

'If you go about quoting Oscar Wilde, John, you won't stay long enough in the service to draw your pension. See you at eight.'

He was prompt, bearing a box of chocolates for Sheila and a bottle of Laphroaig for me.

'I thought you were the one being bribed,' I said.

'No, no. The chocolates are an award to the lady for the plucky and ingenious way in which she extricated herself unharmed from an extremely dangerous situation. The whisky is a consolation for you, for being a big enough idiot to let her get into it.'

'That's a bit hard,' I complained. 'You told her not to be alone.'

'So I did, and you left her alone with a strange taxi driver.'

'Hold on, John,' Sheila interrupted. 'The loony separated us with a trick. Anyone would have fallen for it. I know I would.'

'You, my dear, are an unworldly academic, driven by a thirst to unearth obscure facts which will add to the sum of human knowledge. He is supposed to be an experienced lawyer — versed in the manifold wickednesses of the human heart and mind and always one to pause and consider before making a move.'

'You were a sad loss to the chapel,' I said.

'Not that they thought so at the time,' he said. 'It was their idea that a career in the navy would do me good after my trouble with Sansha Pritchard.'

'You must tell us,' I said.

'That's what they said,' he said. 'What's for dinner?'

Over dinner Sheila gave him the detailed story of the previous night's events. When she had done he asked, 'And you can't recall anything useful about him?'

'I was trying to get away at the time,' she said, 'not drawing pictures.'

'There was,' he said, 'a young lady in Wales, many years ago, who managed to memorise the pattern of a man's teeth while being raped and they got him.'

'Well done her!' said Sheila. 'But my bloke was disguised.'

'You think so?'

'I'm certain. I did actually try to get a look at him, but there was nothing to see — beard, moustache, shades and cap — no face to look at. I remember thinking that at least he wasn't going to kill me.'

'Why's that?'

'Because he wouldn't have disguised himself, would he?'

'True, true. What about his voice? He spoke to you a couple of times.'

'Yes, but nothing very helpful there. It was just posh Pommy, like on the phone.'

'Well,' he said, 'that lets out the usual suspects in crimes of violence — the working class. Anything about him that made you think you could have seen him before?'

She thought for a moment. 'He was too slim for chubby Norman, too tall for Jack Garton or his son and too young for Captain Smythe, if that's what you mean.'

'Which doesn't,' he said, 'mean that he isn't connected with one of the three families you've found.'

'But he used the name Lewis. That's connected with the Stafford man — James Simmonds.'

'True, but he seems to have known very

early on what you were researching. We have to presume he's got much the same information that you have — maybe more. He's certainly got one piece of information that you haven't — he knows what this is all about.'

'Sheila might have that information and not recognise it,' I commented.

'Maybe,' he said. 'Have you got very far with the other families? Like down to the present day?'

'Two of them, I have,' she said. 'I haven't quite sorted out the Shropshire bunch. What help is that? You're not going to go bashing about banging on the doors of my possible contacts, are you?'

'I love,' he said, wearily, 'the graceful way in which the public accepts the efforts of its police officers to keep society safe. No, my love, I wasn't about to go bashing on doors. I was about to see if anyone in the present or previous generation shows up on Criminal Records.'

'Sorry,' she said. 'I'll give you the details I've got so far. I take it all this means that your colleagues over the border didn't catch him and haven't got a clue.'

The big Welshman shook his head. 'No,' he said. 'They didn't get him and they didn't see the car. They reckon that he went on over the moor after you bailed out. Could have fetched up in Sheffield, or he might have reached the motorway through a side-road. Could have gone anywhere. If they'd contacted us a bit quicker I'd have had Belston watched for the car.'

'You think he's hereabouts?' I said.

'I told you that. He knows your comings and goings somehow. He must be fairly close at least some of the time. Anything you remember about the inside of the car, Sheila?'

'Not really.' She frowned. 'There were two of those rings on the dash — you know — the kind you can sit a soft drink can in.'

He nodded. 'Two's unusual. That's something if we ever find the car. What are you doing tomorrow?'

'Ploughing through dross on the Internet again, why?'

'Staffordshire would like you to go up and give them a full statement, if you will.'

'He's not going to try again tomorrow,' she said.

'He's going to try again soon, somehow. What's more, he's getting worse. Dead cats and spiders in wellies are one thing, but kidnap with intent to commit GBH at least is a lot worse. I'll take you up there myself.'

'Does that mean', I enquired, 'that we're

going to have your company for breakfast as well?'

'How very kind,' he said. 'I never thought of that, but I accept — so long as it's a mixed grill. None of your toast and orange juice nonsense.'

'Steak, two eggs and fries do?' asked Sheila.

15

Sheila returned from Stafford next evening in a good mood.

'I have given them a blow-by-blow description of the whole thing,' she said. 'They were honest enough to admit that they didn't know where to start, but John was charming and the young copper who took my statement was really useful.'

'What about the phone numbers — the one in Lewis's letter and the fake taxi number?'

'Two mobiles bought under false names and now switched off,' she said, 'and the address which the letter came from was a fake.'

'Which is why he rushed us into that appointment, so that you weren't going to write back.'

'Still,' she said, 'it wasn't a wasted day. John's right. There are benefits in co-operating with the police. Look at this.'

She produced a piece of paper from her bag and passed it across. It was a photocopy of a Victorian broadsheet.

'My statement,' she said, 'was taken by a very nice sergeant, and when I explained to him how I got into this mess it turned out that he's a local history enthusiast — particularly local criminal history. He told me that he knew about James Simmonds. What's more, he took me to the Salt Library and showed me that. Isn't that great?'

'Very nice,' I said. 'Though I prefer the older sheets, where they have a cheerful picture of a row of blokes dangling from a scaffold at the top.'

'Oh, you!' she said. 'Don't you see what this proves? That Jimmy Simmonds had a girlfriend and a son and it even gives her name.'

'So you've got another candidate for the recipient of the penny. Mrs Wainwright will be most upset.'

'Well, I don't suppose that I'll ever know which girl got the token, but it's really nice to have her name. I wish there was a tune to this song.'

'There is,' I said.

'How do you know?'

'It goes like this,' I said, and hummed it.

She looked at me with a puzzled frown. 'That's too good for you to have just made it up. How do you know it?'

'I don't know the song as such, but those verses are very close to a song called 'Jamie Raeburn's Farewell'.'

A New Song of
JAMES SIMMONDS

My name it is James Simmonds,
In Stafford I was born,
From my place of habitation
I now must leave with scorn,
To leave my loving parents
That grieves my heart full sore,
I am condemned for fourteen years
To far Australia's shore.

So early in the morning
Before the break of day
The warders they awaken us
And to us they do say:
Farewell you hapless felons
We'll never see you more,
This is the day you are to stray
To far Australia's shore!

So we arose, pulled on our clothes,
Our hearts were filled with grief,
Our friends who stood about the gate
Could give us no relief,
Our parents, wives and sweethearts
Whose suffering was full sore,
To see us leave our native land
For far Australia's shore.

Farewell my aged father,
You were the best of men,
And also my own sweetheart
Kate Evans is her name,
We'll kiss beside the pleasant stream
And wander there no more,
For I must leave all that I love
For far Australia's shore.

Farewell my weeping mother,
I'm grieved by what I've done,
I pray God will protect you,
Also my infant son,
Kept always in my aching heart
You shall be evermore,
While I am labouring far away
On far Australia's shore.

148

'And how do you know that?'

'Because my mother was a folk-singer — I've told you that. You know, that's how she bumped into my father, at one of the Edinburgh Fringe shows. Well, I not only inherited her weird library, I also inherited her record collection. That's why I recognise the song.'

'You mean all those old LPs on the bottom shelves? Don't you have to have one of those machines you wind up to play those?'

'Not quite. Go and have a look, somewhere there is a record with 'Jamie Raeburn' on it. It might be a record called *Chorus from the Gallows*.'

She grimaced. 'No wonder it never made the top ten.'

An hour later I went looking for her to tell her dinner was ready. She was sprawled on the sitting-room floor listening to a record.

'Hey! This stuff's bonzer! Why didn't you tell me you had all this great music?'

'I didn't know you liked folk.'

She laughed. 'When I was a kid in Oz, 'folksongs' were what commos and subversives sang — all about downtrodden convicts and heroic bushrangers. There was something called 'Australian traditional song' which was dead boring, and then there was something called 'bush music', which was sung by big, bearded blokes who knew how to drink and that was all about what fun it was being a swaggie out in the desert.'

'The Great Cultural Desert?' I suggested.

'Not so much of it! You're talking about the nation that gave the world Vegemite, *Neighbours* and *Prisoner, Cell Block H*.'

'Not to mention Chips Rafferty, Sidney Bridge and Skippy the Bush Kangaroo.'

She scowled and switched the stereo off. 'Seriously though, did your mum sing all this stuff?'

'A lot of it,' I said. 'She knew a lot of the people on those LPs. She took me to the Newport Festival when I was little. She sang there with Dylan and Baez and everybody, visited Woody Guthrie in hospital and everything.'

'What happened?'

'We came back and found that Captain Flambeau had vanished in a puff of smoke and she devoted her time to raising a brilliant little lawyer.'

'If you had followed in her footsteps,' she said, 'I could have been sleeping with an international superstar. Did you really see Bob Dylan?'

'I think so,' I said. 'I was two at the time. He didn't make a great deal of impact on me. Come and get your dinner.'

After dinner we opened the fan mail. There was not much and none of it was either amusing or useful. There was a small packet, with the label of a computer software firm in London. Sheila turned it over in her hands.

'What's that?' I asked.

'Don't know,' she said. 'I haven't ordered anything.'

'It's probably one of those freebies from an Internet company, guaranteeing you hours of free time if you read all their adverts instead of their competitors.'

'I expect so,' she said, and slit the wrapper open.

'Well,' she said, after reading the leaflets with the CD inside the pack, 'it's a freebie, but it's a bit more specific. It's a genealogical program.'

'You've got one,' I said.

'So I have, but this one is supposed to do everything short of calling Great-Granny back from the dead. I've got to give it a whirl.'

We went through into the study, where Sheila switched on the computer and loaded the disk. The screen came alive with a bright pattern of rising flames.

'What's that got to do with genealogy?' Sheila commented.

'Perhaps Great-Granny didn't go where

everybody expected,' I suggested.

The flames on the screen dropped away to reveal a deep blue sky with a moon and twinkling stars.

'Very pretty,' I said. 'What else does it do?'

Little rockets shot up from the bottom edge of the screen bursting into showers of multi-coloured stars. One large projectile soared to the top of the screen and exploded, showering the entire screen in rainbow-coloured stars, then the screen went black.

'What's happened?' I asked.

'I don't know,' she said, tapping keys.

Nothing happened. The screen stayed blank. No key produced any result. Sheila rapped keys more desperately and muttered in low Australian.

'The damn thing's crashed!' she announced eventually, and switched off the power.

'What now?' I asked.

She took the new disk from the drive and switched on again. 'Try it again,' she said.

The screen remained blank for several seconds, then the pattern of flames appeared again.

'What the hell?' Sheila snarled and then they vanished suddenly, leaving the starlit sky, across which a message appeared:

REMEMBER, REMEMBER,
THE FIFTH OF NOVEMBER.

We had just time to absorb the short legend before the screen darkened again. We waited. Nothing further appeared. Sheila took to the keyboard again, without result. Once more she switched off and on. Nothing happened.

After several minutes she stopped. 'It's wiped everything!' she exclaimed. 'That bloody program has cleared my hard drive. Everything's gone.'

'You mean you've lost all that was on there?'

'It's all gone from the computer, but I've got back-up disks of all of it. It's a damned nuisance. I'll have to reload all my software.'

'What about a thingy — a virus?' I asked. Could it have left one behind?'

She looked thoughtful. 'Yes, it could. I'll have to get Alasdair to take a look at it. What do you think that message meant?'

'It's Guy Fawkes,' I said. 'A kid's rhyme — 'Remember, remember the Fifth of November, gunpowder, treason and plot. Will you tell me a reason why gunpowder treason should ever be forgot.' '

'You don't have to tell a historian about

153

Guy Fawkes, you galah! My dad used to have a bonfire and fireworks. The nuns at school hated it.'

'You know where that disk came from, don't you?'

'Of course I do! It's from bloody Jack the Cat-Ripper, the bastard! But what did he mean? Is he going to do something on November 5th?'

'I shouldn't think so — he doesn't seem to hang about much and that's months away. For all he knows your book might be in print by then. Maybe it's a religious message. Fawkes and his pals were Catholics.'

'Spare me days!' she said. 'Race, money, family pride — how many more motives can this drongo have?'

'It's a threat, anyway,' I said. 'I think he's threatening an explosion. We ought to tell John Parry. And when Alasdair's had at look at the computer, copy all your disks and let me put a set in the office safe.'

'Good thinking,' she said. 'So after he's got us there'll still be a way of finding out who he was.'

'We'll have to stay in at evenings and weekends,' I said. 'He only seems to operate round here when he knows we're out. If we don't go out he may be in difficulties.'

'We can't stay locked up for ever,' she said.

'No, but we don't need to make things any easier for him.'

'It doesn't get any easier,' she said. 'He knows who we are; he knows where we are; he knows when we move and when we don't move. And we haven't got any idea who he is or what it's about.'

'We know where he is,' I said. 'He's somewhere round here. Maybe we can draw him out.'

'Great! And get incinerated in the interests of justice! What are you going to do? Tie me to a tree in the garden and sit on the roof with a shotgun?'

'I'll have to think about it,' I said, 'and talk to John.'

I was still thinking about it in the small hours when Sheila woke up and prodded me.

'Go to sleep!' she commanded.

'I can't,' I said. 'I keep thinking about this madman.'

'Don't worry about him,' she said. 'The worst thing he did was the spider, and he doesn't seem to repeat himself. Spiders scare the bejeesus out of me — men I can deal with,' and she reached between my legs to emphasise her point.

16

There are parts of Wales where the local people are genuinely bilingual. You can hear them dropping in and out of their two languages, sometimes more than once in the same sentence. It drives English listeners crazy. If it was just Welsh they wouldn't expect to understand it, but the mixture of English catches their ear and they wonder why it doesn't make sense.

I'm like that when I hear people talking about computers. At first it seems to make sense, then the bits about 'glitches' and 'handshaking' and 'bauds' and things begin to overwhelm me. On the other hand, my assistant Alasdair loves computers only slightly less than women. His eyes light up if he walks into a room and discovers a dusty old Amstrad PCW and in minutes he'll have taught it to sing in Russian and leap through flaming hoops. Well — not quite, but you know what I mean.

We had handed the sabotage disk to John Parry and invited Alasdair to come and vet Sheila's machine. He had pronounced it clean and free from any virus so we were celebrating over a bottle. Alasdair and Sheila were deep into computer-speak and I was trying to stop my eyes glazing over.

Up to that point I had not told Alasdair about the problems arising from Sheila's research. It didn't seem to touch the office and I had thought that one of us being distracted from working by a loony stalker was enough, but now Sheila had given him the whole story.

'Have you done much of your work through the Internet?' he was asking.

'Yes,' she nodded. 'A few years ago it would have been all hard yakka in dusty archives and libraries, but there's wads of stuff on the Internet that are useful. All the British censuses from the nineteenth century are there. They'll tell you where people lived, what they did for a living, who else lived there, what their relationship was and so on. At 'genuki.org.uk' you can find lists of surnames for a particular county and get in touch with groups and people researching particular names. You can even find nice people who'll go and dig in the dusty archives for you if somebody has to. There's 'rootsweb.com' and the big Mormon database of world-wide records at 'family search.org'. It's a fantastic resource.'

'That might be how he's keeping watch on

you — at least partly,' Alasdair said.

'You mean people's activities on the Internet can be traced?' I asked, suddenly paying attention again.

He nodded. 'There's a lot of sites that can identify you when you come back on to them. That's because, when you first logged on to them, they sent a little text file back to your hard drive. Next time you go back to that site their file — they call it a 'cookie' — tells them who you are. It can also, of course, tell them other things if they want it to. It can be constructed to prowl about your hard drive finding out all sorts of things about you.'

'What a bloody liberty!' Sheila said. 'Can it be stopped?'

'Yes,' he said. 'Quite a lot of people don't like cookies. There's a site at 'www.cookie central.com' that'll tell you all about them and how to stamp on them if you don't like them.'

Sheila pulled a notebook from her shoulder-bag and jotted down the site address.

'But surely,' I said, 'this cookie thing couldn't tell our man when we were in or out and it couldn't tell him that Sheila hates spiders, could it?'

'No,' he agreed. 'Not unless that information was somewhere in your computer. You haven't got a list of pet hates somewhere, have you?'

'Not likely,' she said.

'But would our loony know enough to manipulate a cookie?' I asked.

'He knew enough to set up that disk that crashed the machine. He might even be the operator behind one of the surname sites that Sheila's visited. Anyway, since he cleaned your hard drive there's no cookies in there now. Once you've re-installed your software, go to that cookie site and find out how to crunch them.'

Alasdair wasn't the only one we needed to tell about our problems. If the mystery man was likely to make an explosive attack of some kind, it seemed important to keep Mrs Dunk, who comes in three days a week to clean for me, informed.

Gloria Dunk is the widow of a former regimental sergeantmajor. Local rumour alleges that she married a shy little National Serviceman in the 1950s and drilled him into warrant officer rank and a reputation as the terror of the British Army. Having watched her at work I can believe it. Mrs Dunk believes that resting is a dirty habit, though I found her next morning taking a mug of coffee with Sheila.

'Good morning, Mr Tyroll,' she said.

'Sheila's been telling me about this man who's been bothering her.' Note that, after four years, she still calls me 'Mr Tyroll', but Sheila is on first name terms. The most familiar I've ever dared to be is to shorten her surname.

'Yes, Mrs D,' I said. 'It looks as if he's going to try something that explodes. Now he always seems to do something when he knows we're out, so I don't want anything happening to you by accident.'

'Don't you worry about me,' she said, with a threatening scowl around the kitchen, as though the villain was hiding behind the vegetable rack. 'I shan't stand any nonsense from him.'

'I'm sure you wouldn't,' I said (and I was), 'but he's a sneaky swine and I'd never forgive myself if you came to any harm.'

'Well, I can't get down to my work if I've got to keep one eye over my shoulder all the time,' she complained.

'That's exactly it,' I said. 'How about if you don't come in until we're sure that it's safe? I'll pay you as usual, of course.'

'You don't want to be paying me for nothing,' she said. 'I'm not one to take money for what I'm not doing. There's too much of that about.'

She took a thoughtful swallow of her

coffee. 'I don't know what the world's coming to,' she said. 'When Dunk retired we moved up here because these were nice houses in a quiet area and most of the people were respectable, now it's getting as bad as the town. Did you hear that Mr Hyde got mugged the night before last?'

'No,' I said. 'I don't think I know him.'

'You must do, Mr Tyroll. He's that man with the big moustache and the horn-rims that walks his dog down here every night.'

'What happened?' asked Sheila.

'Well, he stays with my neighbour, Mrs Bradley at number 38. She only has one guest at a time and she's careful about who they are, but she says he's a respectable gentleman. He does reading in Belston Library. He's looking into the life of old Wellinson, the man who started the big iron firm.'

'They've got a big collection of papers about Wellinson at the library,' said Sheila.

Mrs Dunk nodded. 'That's right, and he spends his days there. Mrs Bradley says you wouldn't want a nicer, quieter guest. Well, he came home the other night and he was shaking like a leaf and he had blood all down his face. Mrs Bradley asked what had happened and he said that three young lads had knocked him down as he was walking his dog. It was just about here, you know, by that gully that comes up the side of your garden.'

'Good Lord!' I said. 'Was he badly hurt? Did they steal anything?'

'No,' she said. 'They just knocked him down for fun, it seems. They never tried to take anything. They just ran out of that gully and tumbled him on to the pavement. He had a nasty bruise to his head and his hands was all full of grit from the road.'

'Did he tell the police?' I asked.

'The police!' she snorted. 'What would they do? Here's you not knowing if someone's going to come and bomb you and that John Parry's a friend of yours. He ought to be stopping it. This town is getting like America.'

Another swallow of coffee fuelled her memory. 'And there was Mrs Richards — you've heard me mention her, Mr Tyroll — she was mugged last week.'

'Where was that?' asked Sheila.

'Down the hill, on the Whiteway Road. She was coming home from seeing her sister, about ten o'clock, and the same happened to her as to Mr Hyde. They jumped out of that gully by the White Lion and had her handbag away.'

'Are they both all right?' asked Sheila.

'Well, they'll live,' said Mrs Dunk. 'Mary Richards is a solid body, but Mrs Bradley says that her lodger isn't a well man anyway. He's always drinking tea and he has about six meals a day. He's never said so, but she reckons he's got that, whatdyecallit — you know, Mr Tyroll — where your sugar goes funny?'

'Diabetes,' I said.

'That's right. She says he never puts on weight, but he's always snacking. Takes sandwiches and one of them double Thermos flasks with him to the library.'

If I'd carried on listening, Gloria Dunk would have rehearsed every crime committed in Belston since the Vikings came, but I had an office to run so I left her to Sheila.

That night Sheila asked me about Mrs D's opinions. 'Do you think those kids in the gully might have anything to do with our situation?'

'Do you?' I said. 'Some people know there's a short-cut up from the town and come that way. They were probably doing that and they just came across old whatsisname and his dog.'

'They'll be damned sorry if they try it on with Jack the Cat-Ripper when he's delivering a bomb, won't they?' she grinned.

17

People come to lawyers because they're worried and they expect their lawyer to wipe away all their worries like magic. I can't count the number of times I've told a client, 'Don't worry about it, Mr Bloggs.' 'But I can't help worrying about it,' they say, I give them a confidence-inducing smile, 'I can't stop you thinking about it — that's perfectly natural — but there's really no point in worrying about it. That won't get you anywhere.'

Nor is there and it won't. If you can do something about a situation, then think about it and do whatever it is; if you can't — well, forget about it. So after giving my clients that very sound advice I go home and worry about what I'm going to do about their case. Which is fair enough, really, because that's what my job is. The trouble comes with my own problems. I haven't got anyone to smile warmly at me and say, 'Don't worry about it, Chris Tyroll — it'll all come out right in the end,' and if I did have I probably wouldn't believe them anyway.

The more time that passed after we

received the bomb threat, the more I worried. I didn't care at all for Sheila's image of herself staked out like bait to lure our madman out of the undergrowth, because when he crawled out of the brush he'd be wielding a bomb.

Sheila and I had been bombed before and I didn't much fancy another go. Anyone with any sense has a strong strain of cowardice. Nor did I fancy just sitting around waiting for it to happen. As the days passed and nothing went bang, I got more and more tense. Whether Sheila was equally worried I simply couldn't tell. Much of the time she spent staring at an Internet screen as though it was a crystal ball and would somehow reveal the entire history of all her JS's. Much of my time I spent worrying about our situation instead of my clients' cases, smoking too much and drinking a little extra. Every night, before I had a chance of sleeping, I had to patrol the street, the alley alongside the garden, the back lane and the garden itself. Stupid really, because our maniac had always struck when we were away from home. It wasn't at all likely that I'd bump into him in the alley toting a large black spherical object with a smoking fuse. Still, I had to do it.

I was lying sleepless in bed one night when

my partner poked me in the behind.

'What are you doing on Sunday?' she asked.

'Why? Do you want a date?'

'Not the way you are at the moment,' she said.

'Thanks a million! It may have escaped your notice that I'm somewhat concerned about the real possibility of losing you to the machinations of some explosive nutter!'

'We've been bombed before,' she said.

'If you say that once more, I'll scream,' I said. 'You also appear to have forgotten that last time we ended up being chased across a mountain by a bunch of uniformed banditti with evil intentions towards us.'

'Yair,' she said, 'but we came out of it, didn't we? Anyway, what about Sunday?'

'What about Sunday?'

'I want to go to Shropshire. I think I've tracked down Jonty Sowden's family.'

'The Shrewsbury bloke?' I said. 'Whereabouts in Shropshire?'

'Somewhere called Randstrow.'

'It'll be difficult to get there by train,' I said, 'particularly on a Sunday.'

'I,' she said, 'have persuaded Claude to find us a motor.'

Claude, the Phantom, whose real name is Gordon Raines, is the best private enquiry agent in the Midlands and does a lot of ferreting for me. One of his less savoury occupations is repossessing cars that people haven't paid for, as a result of which he gets first choice when they're sold cheap, though I do occasionally feel guilty about riding in a motor that some poor bloke sweated to pay for and lost to a finance company.

Randstrow turned out to be deep in the heart of Shropshire, well over towards Wales and secreted in a network of deep lanes. Eventually we found Breckberry Farm, a small farmhouse surrounded by well-maintained fields. When we turned into the gate we realised that it wasn't the occupant of Breckberry Farm that tilled those fields. The yard was an empty area of old, broken concrete, spotted with clumps of weeds, and hadn't seen a tractor for years. The vigorous smell of a working farm was entirely absent and the barns and outbuildings were beginning to fall down. Even the dog-kennel by the farmhouse door was untenanted and had no dish beside it.

As Sheila pulled up the farmhouse door opened and a tall, slim man stood there, blinking slightly in the sunlight. Sheila had led me to expect a man in his forties but, at first glance, this man seemed older, mainly because of his severely thinned hair.

He introduced himself as Ian Bradley and led us into the building without offering his hand. Inside it was a typical English farmhouse with a latched door leading off the hall into a large sitting-room that occupied one side of the building. It was low-ceilinged and panelled with match-boarding. One window looked out on a small, unkempt garden and another latched door led to the kitchen. The room was dusty and smelt stale and the furniture was well worn. Despite the warmth of the afternoon it was cold — not just chilly as stone buildings can be, even in summer, but cold as though it was a long time since it had been warm.

Bradley placed us in two armchairs and dropped on to a settee.

'I have to admit,' he said when introductions were over, 'that letter astonished me, Dr McKenna. I hadn't any idea about this person you say was my ancestor. Are you sure you're right?'

He spoke with the soft accent of the Welsh border.

'Pretty certain,' Sheila said, and pulled her file from her shoulder-bag. 'Look,' she went on. 'The man I'm interested in is Jonty Sowden. He was tried at Shrewsbury and shipped out in 1865. Now the census return for 1861 shows a Jonathan Sowden living at Grasslea — that's the next village, isn't it? — and he's not there in the '71 return. In 1861 his age is given as nineteen and my man was twenty-five when he was transported, so it looks like he was the same bloke, doesn't it?'

Bradley nodded. 'It looks like it,' he agreed, 'but how do you connect him with me?'

'Well,' she said, 'Sowden was a single man, so there's no wife or children that I can trace, but the census shows two brothers and a sister, Matilda Elizabeth. I've traced one brother's marriage and his three children. One died in childbirth, one died at the age of ten and the last one lived and died unmarried, so there's no descendants from that branch. The other brother never married but died a bachelor in 1894. The only line of descent I can find is from the sister. Matilda married in 1869 to George Bradley, the tenant of this very farm. Does any of that sound familiar?'

Bradley nodded again. 'It does,' he said. 'My great-great-grandmother was Matilda, but I don't think I ever knew her maiden name.'

'Beauty,' said Sheila. 'We're on the right

track then. Now Matilda and George had only one son, another George, right?'

'Right,' he said. 'My great-grandfather. He married another local girl. My great-grandmother was Emmeline Flowers from Randstrow. They married about 1890 and had one son, my grandfather Jack Bradley.'

'Spot on,' said Sheila. 'I've got John Bradley from the 1891 census return, but after that the returns aren't released yet, so it gets a bit difficult. What happened next?'

'My grandfather,' said Bradley, 'didn't fancy a farming life. He ran off to sea in his teens and knocked about the world a bit. He finally came home just before the Great War.'

'And he was married?' asked Sheila. 'I couldn't find a marriage certificate for him.'

Bradley smiled faintly. 'Oh, yes. He was married. You needn't worry about stumbling on to our family skeleton there. He brought his wife back with him.'

'A Spanish lady?' asked Sheila. 'I've got the name Consuela from your father's birth certificate, but there's no place of birth.'

'No.' He shook his head. 'Not Spanish, Dr McKenna — Venezuelan. After being at sea for a while, Grandad fetched up in South

America and that was where he met his bride.'

'Do you remember her?'

'Not very well. She died quite young, you know, in her fifties, while I was still very small. My mother told me that Grandma went a bit funny in her later years.'

Sheila had been jotting notes on a shorthand pad. She made another and then went on.

'And you father — Edward Bradley — was an only son?'

'Yes. My grandad served in the navy in the Great War and when he came home it seemed to have finished his wanderlust. He settled down quietly and ran the farm. My father was born in 1920 and he grew up to run the farm as well.'

'But you don't?' said Sheila.

'No, no,' he said. 'Even if I had wanted to, my arthritis wouldn't let me now. But before we get to me, can I offer you both coffee?'

'How nice,' said Sheila. 'Can I help you make it?'

She rose and dropped her notepad into my lap. As Bradley showed her through to the kitchen I looked at the top sheet on the pad. Scrawled across it was a command:

TAKE A QUICK SQUID IN THE DRAWERS
TO YOUR LEFT.

I had no idea what prompted the message, but on the basis that the coffee might be instant I had to move quickly. To my left was a nondescript sideboard with two cupboards topped by two drawers. Standing up, I pulled each drawer out quickly, glimpsed the contents and shut them, then did the same for each of the cupboards.

I moved quickly across to a large bookcase, fronted with unpolished glass. It was impossible to find a theme in the books on the shelves. There were textbooks of physics and chemistry, an English grammar, a history of jazz, the Opies' *Lore and Language of Schoolchildren*, a book on recreational maths, a Dutch grammar, a biography of Chopin, a volume of local ghost stories, a range of modern novels from about the 1940s down to the '70s and a shelf of boy's adventure stories — Stevenson, Buchan, Dumas and the like.

I was still standing in front of the case when Sheila and Ian Bradley returned from the kitchen. It's absolutely not on to sneak a peek into a man's drawers and cupboards when you're a guest in his house, but for some reason it's quite all right to pore over his selection of books. Some people believe that you can tell a lot about someone by the books they keep, but Bradley's shelves only confused me.

'Not all mine,' he said, when he saw what I was doing. 'The novels mostly belonged to my late mother.'

He sat down and Sheila doled out coffee from a tray. I saw why Bradley had not shaken hands on our arrival, when he took his coffee from Sheila in a large mug, holding it between two clenched hands that trembled slightly.

Sheila sat down, took a long draught of coffee and delved into her shoulder-bag.

'So you definitely are the present generation of Jonty Sowden's family,' she said. 'I've got his convict records here.'

Bradley smiled his faint smile. 'I'm not just the present generation of the family,' he said. 'I'm the last generation.'

'You're not married?' said Sheila, though both of us had concluded that shortly after arriving.

'No,' he said. 'I've never been married. It never seemed to be the right time for it.'

He picked up the photocopies of Sowden's records and scanned them.

JONTY SOWDEN No 6913
tried 12th June 1865,
arrived Fremantle Barracks March 1866.
Born 2nd January 1846

Trade: Farm labourer Height: 5ft. 7 in.
Complexn: Fair Head: Medium
Hair: Fair Whiskers: Small fair
  moustache
Visage: Round Forehead: M.Ht
Eyebrows: Fair Eyes: Grey
Nose: Medium Mouth: Wide
Chin: Rounded Remarks: 4 in. scar
  on r.thigh, tattoo
  r.upper arm —
  Crown & Anchor.

Convict 7 years' transportation
Tried at Shrewsbury, transported for arson
Character: Fair

He shook his head slowly. 'I never heard anything about him,' he said. 'I suppose they were ashamed of him. Particularly the Bradleys — they were real respectable farmers, never put a foot out of line. Do you know exactly what he did?'

'No,' said Sheila. 'I haven't checked the trial records yet, but arson in the countryside in the last century was usually political, wasn't it? Rick-burning and that?'

'It might have been,' he agreed. 'That did

happen round here more than once.'

Sheila sipped at her coffee. 'You were going to tell us about yourself, Mr Bradley,' she said.

18

'There's not much that would interest you,' he said. 'As you know, my father was Edward Bradley. Unlike Grandad, my father stuck to the farm and led a dull but worthy life. He expected me to do the same, but I'm afraid I wasn't cut out for it. I had other things in mind.'

'What were they?' I asked.

'Music,' he said. 'I was crazy about music when I was young. I couldn't get enough of it, of any kind. Mother used to say that I got it from my grandmother. Apparently she was a singer when Grandad met her in South America, but I didn't sing. I played any instrument I could get my hands on.'

He pointed into the shadows at the darker end of the room, away from the window. An old-fashioned, robust upright piano stood there. I thought about his hands now, hands that he couldn't or wouldn't open.

'My mother bought the best instrument she could afford, and made sure I had lessons. Then I went on to the guitar, and wind instruments and strings. I may not have been equally expert on all of them, but I could get a melody out of almost anything. And I played any kind of music. My teens were in the late 1950s — rock and roll, the jazz revival, country music — I played them all, as well as the classics.'

He paused and gazed away out of the window, his hands trembling more vigorously.

'By the time I left school I knew I wasn't a farmer. I had terrible rows with my father about it, but I knew it had to be music. When he wouldn't let me go on to study any kind of music, I ran away. There must have been a bit of my grandad in me, as well as my grandmother.'

'How old were you?' asked Sheila.

'I was sixteen,' he said. 'Everybody knows everything at sixteen. I had a good time actually. It was the Swinging Sixties, there was a lot of music about, and once people found I could play I could always find a home and an income. I wandered about, not just Britain, but Europe as well. I spent a long time in Amsterdam. I mixed with all sorts of people. I could write you a book about the real sixties, about sex and drugs and rock and roll and petty crime and booze. But you grow up in the end — if you're lucky you do.'

He paused and lifted his coffee mug with his awkward two-handed grip. 'I grew up when I realised something very important.'

'What was it?' asked Sheila.

'I realised one day that I was a good instrumentalist on three or four instruments and a passable player on half a dozen more — but there was no instrument on which I was outstanding. I was a good session man, in rock, in pop, in jazz, in the classics; I was a useful member of a band or an orchestra, but I was not a soloist. I simply didn't have whatever it is that makes some people's music ring out and catch the hearts of an audience so that they can't hear anyone else.'

'What did you do?' said Sheila, quietly.

'Do? Don't you know what they say? Those who can, do; those who can't, teach. I came home. I did not even know that my father had died of pneumonia while I was away. There was no farm any more. My mother had sold off the land and just kept the buildings. There was money from the land, so I could go to college, and I trained as a teacher.'

Awkwardly he lifted his mug again.

'I went to work in a private school. I taught maths and science and music. Maths comes easily to some musicians but it was the music that I took the job for. I taught the boys, I conducted the orchestra and trained the choir and I loved it. I really think I'd found what I was meant to be — someone who could spot and nurture a talent that might one day be the soloist I never was.'

'And did you spot any?' I asked.

'One, at least, one definitely. He'll be great someday.'

He smiled at the recollection, then shook his head as though to clear it away.

'The rest I'm sure you can guess, Dr McKenna. I developed arthritis in my hands. I cannot play an instrument of any kind any more, so my musical years are over.'

He said it without apparent bitterness, but his face belied his tone.

'That's why I said I'm the last of the Bradley's. When it gets worse I shall have to leave here. Did you know this farm has been in the Bradley family for two hundred and fifty years? Well, I shall have to move when I get beyond helping myself and that won't be very long.'

He stopped and stared past us again. The silence stretched. His trembling had increased.

'I'm sorry,' he said at last. 'You didn't come here to listen to my troubles, did you? But I'm afraid I haven't given you much to write about. Just a family of farmers ending with a former session man and music teacher. Nothing very exciting there. It looks like whatsisname — Jonty Sowden — was the most exciting member of the family, except maybe Grandpa.'

With difficulty he heaved himself off the settee and crossed to the sideboard by my chair. One of the drawers had been filled with bottles of pills. He took a bottle out and fumbled it open, dropped two capsules on to the top of his clenched fist and swallowed them.

Sheila got up and signalled to me to follow.

'I think we've taken up too much of your time,' she said. 'You were very kind to see us and help me.'

'I don't think I can have helped you very much, Dr McKenna.'

'Well,' she said, 'once I've confirmed that I've got the right families I shall research them back as far as possible so as to try and give as complete a picture as possible.'

He dropped the pill bottle back in the drawer and shut it.

'It's been a pleasure meeting you,' he said. 'And quite novel, learning that someone in my family was transported. Perhaps he was like Grandad and me — didn't fancy life on the land.'

'I don't suppose he intended to get transported,' Sheila said.

He gave his thin smile. 'No,' he said. 'Suppose not.'

We were silent for a while once we got into

the car. The sad, lonely man in his dusty, cold farmhouse had brought us both down.

'Pub?' queried Sheila, after a few miles.

'Why not?' I said and we were soon settled behind a table in the back garden of a village pub, sandwiches and drinks on the table.

'All right,' she said. 'Come clean! What was in the drawers?'

'You saw what was in the drawer,' I said. 'Medicines.'

'One drawer,' she said. 'Give!'

'Only if you tell me why you wanted me to look.'

'Because the top of that sideboard had something standing on it which he put away before we came. You could see the lines in the dust. My guess is two photo frames, one single and one double. I just wanted to know what he was hiding from us.'

'Spot on, Sherlock,' I said. 'The right-hand drawer had two photo frames in it — one double and one single. The double had pictures of a young blonde woman with a baby — '

'Taken when?' she demanded.

'Hold on, hold on. About mid-seventies, I'd guess. The single had a professional shot of a boy about fourteen. White shirt and bow tie, sitting by a piano and smiling at the

181

photographer. Maybe a print of a newspaper picture.'

'Taken when?' she demanded again.

'Difficult to tell. He was all dressed up for some event. Quite recent, I think.'

'Was he the baby in the other photo?

'I don't know. Have a heart, I only took a quick glance and they all look alike as babies — boys look like Winston Churchill and girls look like Queen Victoria.'

'And I kept Bradley in the kitchen as long as I could, to give you plenty of time. I couldn't ask him to bake us a bloody cake, could I?'

'Well, now you know what was in there what does that tell you?'

'That he wasn't coming clean about not being married.'

'He might have been. That may have been somebody else's wife, or a girlfriend. It might be someone else's baby.'

'Come on!' she said. 'How many blokes do you know who keep photos of someone else's rug-rats? And what about the piano picture? Is that somebody else's kid?'

'That might be his prize pupil,' I said.

'Oh yair!' she said. 'I thought people had caught on to school-teachers who got fond of the pupils. You mark my words — he's got a wife and at least one kid somewhere.'

'They might be dead,' I suggested.

'He said he'd never been married. He's got a wife. He'd have told us if they were dead.'

'He might feel it's too personal.'

'He didn't mind telling us about his wild youth and his frustrated ambitions — why should he mind telling us about a dead wife and kid? No, Chris, Bradley's got a wife and kid somewhere.'

'And I suppose you're going to find them?'

'Too right I am.'

'Hang about a bit,' I said. 'Aren't you in danger of invading Bradley's privacy?'

She snorted. 'I'm not going to write about anything that'll embarrass him. I just want to know the truth. If it's simply that he divorced her because she's tone deaf, or she divorced him because he played his ocarina in the bedroom, that's their business.'

I've learnt not to argue with Sheila unless it's important and I'm right. Even then I quite often lose, so I tried to change the subject.

'Hold on,' she commanded. 'You haven't told me what was in the cupboards.'

'You didn't ask me to look in the cupboards.'

'Don't come the raw prawn with me! Of course you looked in the cupboards.'

'All right! They were both stacked with

183

sheet music. Anything suspicious there? After all, the guy's a former pro musician and teacher.'

After that she let me change the subject.

It was well after dark when we got home. I left Sheila sitting in the car while I inspected the house inside and out. There was nothing there. Once we were both inside Sheila put coffee on while I picked up the messages from the telephone answering machine. The last one was from John Parry.

'Chris?' he said. 'Sheila? This is John calling at 16.45 on Sunday afternoon. Whenever you get in, ring me on my mobile,' and he added the number. He sounded serious. I picked up the phone.

19

There are some police officers you can trust and some you can't. In my job you meet too many of the second kind. You usually find out which is which in the witness box. I met John Parry in the witness box, nearly ten years ago — at least, he was in the witness box. We had a little exchange about the arrest of one of my clients.

'It says in your statement, sergeant, that when my client answered the door, you handed him a sheaf of thirty-two summonses. Is that right?'

'Yes, sir.'

'And what did he say?'

He paused and looked as though he was trying to remember. 'I can't rightly recall, sir.'

'Let me help you, sergeant. Did he not say, 'Fuck me, sergeant! I'll need bleeding Perry Mason to get me out of this lot!' '

John Parry paused again then, deadpan, he said, 'Yes, sir. I do believe that those are the exact words he said.'

'And might I ask why they are not recorded in your statement?'

'Only because I didn't think anyone would believe them, sir.'

After that we got to know each other and I developed a great affection for the big Welshman. I never saw him give way to anger (though I was told that he could, and did) and I never saw him deal with crises with anything other than a heavy Celtic irony.

When he arrived at my home that night he had a folder tucked under his arm and he looked more serious than I could recall. As I opened the door to him he said, urgently, 'Did you search the place when you got home?'

'Yes,' I said.

'And the garden?'

'Yes — and the garden. All quiet.'

'Nothing delivered while you were out?'

I shook my head. 'No. Look, what is this all about?'

'You know what it's all about,' he said. 'Where's Sheila?'

'She's in the kitchen. Making coffee.'

'Good. I'll go and help her drink it,' he said and strode through to the kitchen.

'Good-day, John,' she greeted him. 'What brings you out on a Sunday night?'

'The smell of coffee,' he said.

She poured the coffee and all three of us sat around the kitchen table.

'All right, John,' I said. 'What's on your mind?'

'Where have you two been?' he said.

'We've been in the wilds of Shropshire,' I said, and outlined our day for him.

'There's been an incident at the Royal Mail sorting office in Wolverhampton,' he said.

'What happened?' I asked. 'Put an envelope in the right bag for a change, did they?'

'No joke,' he said. 'They had a fire last night.'

'A fire!' Sheila said.

'Yes,' he said. 'A package caught fire in one of the sorting bins.'

'What? Spontaneously?' I asked.

'No,' he said. 'It was specially devised by the sender to catch fire.'

'And you think it was meant for me?' asked Sheila.

'I don't think, Sheila. I know it was meant for you.'

'You'd better tell us about it,' I said.

'In the early hours of this morning,' he said, 'one of the sorting bins at Wolverhampton burst into flames. Well, there were a few people working near it and fire extinguishers handy, so they had the fire out very quickly, but when they looked to see what had caused it they thought they'd better call in West Midlands police. They had a look and decided it was an arson device.'

'A fire-bomb?' I said.

'That's it. It was a package wrapped in one of those padded envelopes, a bit bigger than A5 and about half an inch thick. The Post Office lads had put it out so quickly that quite a lot of it survived. The police could see how it was meant to go off and what had gone wrong.'

'And that was?'

'Well, there's various ways of detonating a letter-bomb, some of them quite complicated, some quite simple. You can do it with the banger out of a Christmas cracker if you know how, but this was a bit more complicated. The body of the package was sheets of newspaper that had been impregnated with a combustible chemical and dried out. In between two layers of that was the ignition device embedded in a layer of chemicals. That had a sort of spring-loaded button on top that stuck up through a hole in the top layer of paper. When the button was released it fired a little charge and set the paper off.'

'That sounds quite complicated,' I said. 'How was it set?'

'He must have pressed the button down and held it with his fingers while he slid it into the padded envelope, then held it in

position while he put enough paper underneath it to jam it up against the top of the
envelope and stop it going off.'

'Dodgy,' I said. 'It might have gone off in
his hands.'

'And what a pity that would have been!'
said Sheila.

'When he'd got it in place,' John went on,
'he sealed the envelope and strapped it well
with sticky tape, to keep the pressure on the
ignition button.'

'So what went wrong?' I asked.

'It looks as if it got folded across the
middle somewhere in the post, before it was
slung in the sorting bin. Then something else
was thrown in and moved it. It unfolded and
released the button, so it caught fire.'

'Nasty,' said Sheila. 'And I was meant
to . . . '

'You were meant to slit the envelope and
start to pull out the papers. As soon as the
pressure on the button decreased the whole
thing would have gone pop. At the very least
you'd have had badly burned hands and
possibly your face, and there's another thing.'

'What's that?' she said.

'The chemicals had been mixed with soap
flakes.'

'Soap flakes?' I said. 'What was that for? A
whiter than white bomb?'

'No,' he said. 'They melt in the explosion and stick to whatever they touch, so that they make it burn.'

'That sounds pretty sophisticated,' I said, thinking about an explosion of flame scattering sticky, burning droplets around it.

'The West Midlands bomb boys said it was ingenious but not made by a professional,' he agreed.

'Well,' said Sheila, 'at least I haven't got the Continuity IRA or the Basque Separatists after me. Anyway how do you know it was for me?'

He opened his folder and took out some A4 laser copies of colour photographs. They were close-ups of the charred remains of the packet. The address label had been laser printed, so that beyond the charred area the rest could be read clearly:

> ENNA,
> Y ROAD,
> TON,
>   LANDS.

'Dr Sheila McKenna, 55 Whiteway Road, Belston, West Midlands,' I recited.

John nodded. 'That's right. As soon as West Midlands saw it was for Belston they got on to us. Not many names that end in E-N-N-A, so it didn't take long to tie it up with a certain

190

Aussie who was being targeted by a nutter.'

'How did they know it wasn't Wolverhampton?' she demanded.

'The town name is too short, isn't it?' he said.

'Which brings us to where it was sent from,' I said. 'Any ideas?'

'Sadly, no,' he said. 'If you look at the remains of those strips of transparent tape on this side of the envelope, you'll see that they would have passed right over the area of the stamps, so that the postmark ink wouldn't take and it would get wiped off. He wasn't taking any chances, but it got burned off anyway.'

'Any ideas from the bits of newspapers?' I asked.

'Ah, Sherlock Holmes stuff — 'By examining the typeface I can see that this came from the early West Highland edition of the *Scotsman* and was cut out by a short-sighted, red-headed man with a squint and two gold teeth, Watson.' No such luck. All the surviving bits are from the *Independent*.'

'Well,' I said, 'that narrows it down to about a quarter of a million.'

'And their cleaners and their landladies and their friends and their kids,' he said gloomily.

'Fingerprints?' I suggested.

'Have a heart, boyo. No self-respecting villain has left fingerprints since the Great War. Only the amateurs and the idiots. Whatever our man is, he isn't an idiot.'

'But the remains were checked for prints?' I persisted.

'Yes, and there aren't any.'

'But', I said, 'you said he had to hold that button down hard while he slid the device into the package, then keep holding it while he pushed more paper underneath it. Then he taped the envelope tightly and stamped it.'

'Yes,' he said. 'So what?'

'So, he managed all that without leaving prints?'

He stared at me wide-eyed for a moment, then said with exaggerated patience, 'Because he wore gloves, boyo, I told you.'

'So his prints may be on file, then. That's what I was trying to say. If he went to that much trouble to conceal them, maybe he knows they're on record.'

'Right, right. That could be, but I checked all the suspects that Sheila listed for me. All those who might be alive and a few who turned out to be dead. Nobody.' He shook his head. 'No convictions among them, apart from motoring and one for not paying a National Insurance contribution. Got any more suspects, Sheila? What about this bloke you've been to see today?'

'Bradley?' I said. 'He taught science. He'd know how to make it, but he couldn't even lift a coffee mug properly because of his arthritic hands. I can't see him painstakingly putting that bomb together.'

'No,' he said, 'I suppose not.'

'So you're really no further forward?' I said.

'Oh yes,' he said. 'We now know that he means it when he threatens, we know he's escalating the violence, and we know that he's changed his pattern.'

'In what way?' said Sheila.

'Because he's always acted in person before. He could just as well have walked up your garden and dropped his bomb through a window with a timer instead of his press button, but he didn't — he sent it by post, even though you were away. Why was that?'

'Perhaps he was away from Belston as well,' suggested Sheila. 'After all, he can't sit around all the time, watching us. Presumably he has to do other things.'

John nodded. 'Yes, and it would have been nice to know where this came from,' he said, rapping the photographs. 'This man worries me.'

'He's not giving Chris and me a lot of joy,' said Sheila.

'I don't suppose,' he said, 'but what worries me is that this is the first time he's got it wrong. What'll he do now? Will he try the same trick again? Or a variation? I don't like the thought of him trying harder. You could have been badly burned or blinded by this thing. What's he going to try next?'

He left us with that gloomy thought. In bed later we both lay and smoked.

'Penny for them?' said Sheila after a while.

'It was a penny that got us into this,' I said. 'I was just thinking about what John said. What'll he try next?'

'No point in worrying about it,' she said. 'All we can do is be careful.'

'You're not worried?'

'Of course I'm worried, you great galah! But what can we do? I'm not going to stop. Even if I did we don't know that he'd believe it. How could we tell him, anyway? Take an ad in the *Independent*?'

She smoked silently again for a while, then, 'Bradley,' she said.

'What about him? He's not a bomb-maker.'

'So you said, but I'm not sure.'

'Why not? What about his hands? If he can't play an instrument or hold a cup, he'd never risk mucking about with that bomb.'

'I suppose not, but suppose he hasn't got arthritis?'

'Why do you say that? You saw the way he was with his hands.'

'Yes, right, but when he got up to get his pills I noticed something. He spread both hands open on the arm of the settee as he levered himself up. If his hands are that bad, that'd hurt like hell.'

'He was trembling like a leaf,' I said.

'He was doing that all the time. It just got worse. I'm going to have a dig into Mr Bradley and his mysterious photos. Do you think John could find out about him?'

'Probably, but don't ask him. It's illegal. Get Claude to do it for you.'

20

We were cautious about opening the post next day, as John Parry had warned us to be, but there were no further bombs. Only a white envelope with a printed label, exactly like the one on the incendiary package. Inside was a single slip of paper with a message:

MCKENNA, MCKENNA,
FLY AWAY HOME.
THINGS WILL START BURNING
AND SOON YOU'LL BE ONE.

' 'Soon you'll be one,' ' Sheila read. 'Does that mean the package wasn't meant to catch me?'

'No. It means that, if you hadn't been burned by his damned parcel, you soon would be. That means that, as soon as he finds out you weren't caught, he'll try again.'

Things weren't much better at the office. My first client of the day was Sawney. The Crown Prosecution Service had supplied a summary of their case and a copy of the statement which he was alleged to have made.

'Look,' I said 'I've got a copy of the

statement here that they say you made.'

I read it to him: 'I have been cautioned and told that I do not have to say anything but that if I do not now mention anything which I later rely on in my defence it may be to my disadvantage. I wish to make a statement and I want someone to write it down. For six months I have lived in a boarding house at 43 Sandyway Lane, Belston. I occupy a single bed-sitter on the second floor. On the same floor is a room occupied by a woman in her twenties who is called Jane Gardner. We have become friends and sometimes visit each other in our respective rooms. On the first floor a man called Thomas lives in a bed-sitter at the back. I do not know his full name. Thomas is his surname. He works for the Council. Some weeks ago he bought a stereo radio/cassette machine. I remember that he showed it to us in the lounge on the day that he bought it. It looked like quite an expensive machine. I have been out of work for some time and I was short of money. One night I was in Jane Gardner's room and she mentioned the radio/cassette that Thomas had bought and said something about him not being short of money. I said to her that if his radio/cassette was stolen I could sell it. She said that he was careless and sometimes left his door unlocked when he went to work.

I told her to keep her eyes open and see when he left his door unlocked so that she could steal his radio/cassette. A few days later she invited me into her room and showed me the radio/cassette which she had hidden under the bed. I told her that she should keep it hidden in her room and that I would find someone to buy it. I am sorry now that I led her into stealing the radio/cassette. I have made this statement consisting of two pages of my own free will. I have read it over and I have been told that I can add, alter or delete anything which . . . '

I looked up. 'That last bit,' I said, 'the caption, as they call it, appears to be written in your handwriting. After that it's signed, by you and by two police officers, Sergeant Brown and Constable Allen. Is it true?'

'What do you mean, 'Is it true?' Do you mean are the facts true, or do you mean did I make that statement?'

'Either,' I said.

'It isn't true and I don't know if I made it.'

I sighed and turned the document around on the desk. 'Have a look at the writing, Mr Sawney,' I invited. 'Is that last bit written in your handwriting and is that your signature at the bottom?'

He took a pair of glasses from his breast pocket and peered at the paper for a long time. At last he said, 'I don't know. It might be my writing, but it can't be true.'

'Why not?'

'I told you, Mr Tyroll. I can't read handwriting, but it says here that I'd read it over. I couldn't have done that.'

'Are you saying that you did make this statement, but that you didn't read it over?'

'I don't know.'

'How come you don't know?'

'I told you before,' and the note of indignation in his voice was rising to a hysterical pitch, 'I really can't recall what happened at the police station'

'Why is that?'

'It's just some kind of a blank. I might have had an epileptic attack.'

'Do you have epilepsy? You mentioned that last time.'

'I had brain damage in a car accident, Mr Tyroll. I have fainting spells — black-outs.'

'Did you black out in the police station?'

He shook his head. 'I really don't know. Sometimes I can't remember when I've had one.'

'Are you being treated for this? Do you have medication?'

'My doctor gives me pills for the fainting spells.'

'What are they supposed to do? Do they

prevent them, or are they for afterwards?'

'He says that they reduce the frequency of the attacks but I'll still have them if I'm very upset or strained. I was very upset at the police station.'

'Do you carry your medication on you?'

'Yes, usually, in case I have an attack.'

'Have you got it on you now?'

'Well, no. I didn't think you were going to upset me, Mr Tyroll.'

Or he'd just invented the idea of medication, I didn't know. I summed up.

'So, when you were arrested you would have been carrying your pills?'

'I expect so, yes.'

'And when you were interviewed you might have blacked out?'

'Yes.'

'And you may have written the caption on the statement and signed it?'

'Well, I think I remember copying something out from a card.'

'But you don't recall making the statement while PC Allen wrote it down?'

'No.'

'And what it says about you and Jane Gardner and the radio/cassette — is that bit true?'

'Certainly not. I wasn't particularly friendly with her. I asked her out, but she refused. I was never in her room, ever.'

'They've got a statement from her saying exactly the same as yours — that you suggested she steal the radio so that you could sell it. Why did she say that if it's not true?'

'I don't know. Perhaps she doesn't like me, but she's got no reason.'

Not much, I thought. 'Well then,' I said, 'you'd better tell me who your doctor is, so that I can get a medical report.'

The address he gave me was in Warwickshire.

'That's the other side of Brum,' I remarked.

'Dr Glenn is my family doctor,' he explained. 'He's known me since I was a child.'

'Tell him he'll be hearing from me with a request for a medical report. You'd better sign one of these consent forms.'

He signed the form and left. I dictated a letter to Dr Glenn and tried to forget him but no day is long enough to forget Sawney.

Sheila, by contrast, was full of bounce when I got home, bringing me a drink almost before I was through the door.

'Do I owe you any money?' I asked, suspiciously. 'Or do you want to borrow some?'

'Oh, cheers to you, you miserable Pommy wowser!' she said. 'I take it you've had a hard day at the office?'

'No, but I had Sawney in to see me first thing, and I'm getting lost in his evasions. You, I take it, have had an absolutely splendid day?'

'Too right,' she said. 'This morning I rang John Parry and told him about the letter, so he came round and collected it to take it away to be forensicked.'

'And we all know what they're going to find;' I said, 'Absolutely nothing. Laser print, which can't be identified, on cheap chain store stationery which can be bought all over Britain, and no fingerprints.'

'That's what he said,' she agreed, 'but this one did have a postmark.'

'Did it?' I said. 'I was too taken up with the message this morning to notice. What was it?'

'Belston,' she said.

'So he probably posted the fire-parcel in Belston as well.'

'Not necessarily.'

'Well, it would be pretty pointless to post them both in separate places. Anyway, why are you so pleased that we now know that our nutter hangs about Belston — which we knew before — and nothing else?'

'It wasn't that. I had a late breakfast with

John and we talked about my research.'

'Oh yes! I'm slaving away over wretched clients and you're living it up with friendly coppers.'

'He's not my type,' she said. 'I prefer little dark blokes like you.'

'Only because you know you can beat me up.'

'Very likely,' she said, 'but anyway, John says they've got a police museum in Birmingham that's got a huge collection of photographs of Victorian villains, going right back into the 1850s.'

'But you haven't got a JS from Brum, have you?'

'Oh yes I have. Jack Sullivan. He was tried at Warwick, but he lived in Birmingham.'

'Of course,' I said. 'They still commit cases from the Chelmsley Wood area of Brum to the Warwick Crown Court.'

'So I rang the museum,' she continued, 'and a very nice man there said that he'd got what might be a photo of my Jack Sullivan before he was transported.'

'That's amazing,' I said. 'What's more, I think that Warwick Crown Court still sits in an eighteenth-century court-house and uses the old original octagonal courtroom where Jack Sullivan would have been told the bad news.'

'Really?' she said. 'Why octagonal?'

'There's an octagonal chamber underneath the dock, with stairs up the middle into the dock, and eight sets of irons in the angles of the walls. When things were very busy, they could weigh them off faster by starting the day with eight prisoners in the hold under the dock, then feeding them fast up the stairs to be sorted out. The place was obviously designed by a time-and-motion man.'

She grimaced. 'You lot really took this populating the new colony seriously, didn't you?'

I refused to rise to her bait. 'What's for dinner?' I enquired hopefully.

'Nothing,' she said. 'It's your turn.'

I groaned.

'Never mind,' she said. 'Neck that drink and I'll bring you another while I take over the cooking.'

'Bless you!' I said, and I meant it. 'So, what's for dinner?'

'Goat or galah,' she announced.

'Galahs talk, don't they? I don't think I could face a talking dinner.'

'Have to be goat, then.'

The goat turned out to be duck in plum sauce, which almost expunged the recollection of Mr Sawney.

'So,' I said, when I was lolling back

overstuffed, with another glass in front of me, 'when are we going to this police museum?'

'I,' she said, emphasising the pronoun, 'am going tomorrow.'

'I can't go tomorrow.'

'You don't need to go,' she said.

'Do you think it's a good idea — going alone?'

'For heaven's sake!' she snapped. 'It's at the Police Training Centre. The place is probably crawling with coppers.'

'And how will you know whether one of them is Jack the Cat-Ripper? Anyway, it's a museum, most of the coppers will be stuffed ones, with top hats and rattles. I was merely trying to follow John Parry's advice.'

'You were merely trying to imply that I'm not safe out on my own. Kindly remember that it took your help to get me kidnapped!'

'That', I said, 'is not fair.'

'True, though.'

'Look, I just don't think you ought to be . . . '

' . . . wandering about helplessly in the big wide world without a bodyguard,' she finished. 'I am going — tomorrow — alone.'

'You look wonderful when you're angry,' I said.

'That's not even original,' she said. 'It's Louis Hayward to Joan Bennett in *Son of*

205

Monte Cristo, about sixty years ago — and it probably wasn't original then, and it's not true now. When I'm angry, I'm angry — and I'm angry, Chris Tyroll!'

With which she made a dramatic and door-rattling exit, leaving me wondering what I'd done to bring that on. It occurred to me — rather too late — that I spent a lot of time worrying about how I felt about the threat against Sheila and probably not enough time worrying about how she felt about it.

21

For some women, nagging is a substitute for sex. My ex-wife was an Olympic standard nagger. The year that I told her she couldn't go Christmas shopping in New York she bent my ear at every available opportunity, including all our friends' Christmas parties, for a straight month, with occasional replays all the way up to our divorce eighteen months later. Still, it's some kind of a relationship, I suppose.

Sheila, as I might have guessed, was different. She was the silent type. The day after our spat she went to the police museum — on her own. I was already at home when she came back. We had a brief conversation.

'How was the museum?' I asked, in as neutral a tone as I could muster.

'Absolutely dreadful,' she said, with complete conviction. 'I was attacked by a herd of rampaging rhinoceroses and had to be rescued by a boy scout!'

So I shut up, and we stayed that way for three days, confining ourselves to 'Please pass the salt' conversations. I know lots of couples go through these periods, but lots of couples don't have an unknown, clever, violent loony after them. It was not a very good time at all and we both drank a lot.

We were at breakfast in the kitchen one morning. I was flipping through the morning paper and wondering if this deadlock was going to last until Sheila went back to Australia in the following spring, when the postman arrived.

Sheila fetched some letters and a package to the table. If relations had been normal I would have looked at the package with her and tried to work out whether it was too risky to open. As it was I looked across, saw a shallow, rectangular parcel, noted the 'West Midlands Police Museum' label on which the address was written and left her to it.

Sheila had taken a knife to the brown tape sealing the end of the envelope. As she turned the packet in her hands I glimpsed a flash of bright colour. She had already inserted the point of the knife, but I reached across, snatched the packet from her hand and flung it into the sink, catching her hand and trying to drag her down behind the table as I did so.

We had just reached the floor amid a welter of spilled coffee and broken crockery when the sink erupted. I thought the world had blown up. A loud, sharp explosion hit my ear-drums like a blow from a cricket bat — in stereo. Dust blew up from the sink in a grey fountain that drifted all over the room. Sheila and I lay on the floor, stunned, our ears ringing like a carillon from the blast. It was probably a loud crash, but it sounded like a soft thud when the bottom of the sink fell out on to the tiled floor. After that everything went quiet — apart from the ringing noise — while we lay and shook all over.

How long it was before we pulled ourselves together sufficiently to crawl up from the floor and cough our way to the phone I don't know. The explosion's impact had left me feeling totally gutted and weakened. Severe shock, I suppose, though you shouldn't really be shocked when something you think is a bomb goes bang.

We had barely time to wipe the crust of grey dust from our faces and pour ourselves a stiff drink before John Parry was with us. While his subordinates swarmed over the kitchen, we sat out in the garden, cautiously sipping whisky and trying to tell him what had happened. That wasn't easy. Neither of us could hear properly and John had to ask his questions slowly and loudly in order to make himself understood.

'What did you think the package was?' he asked Sheila.

'I followed up your tip,' she said. 'I went to

the police museum and they were going to send some copies of photographs. That's what I thought it was. It had a label on it — 'West Midlands Police Museum'.'

He nodded. 'And what made you suspicious?' he asked me.

'Like Sheila, I thought it was OK at first. Then I caught a glimpse of the stamps. I suddenly thought that was wrong — it should have been franked, not stamped.'

'And,' he said, wearily, 'instead of leaving it on the table and summoning your friendly neighbourhood policeman, you elected to fling it in the sink, where it went off.'

'Sheila had already started to slit it open,' I said. 'I thought it would go off anyway.'

'Was there a particular reason why you were both being bloody careless and not paying attention?'

'We had had a little falling out,' I said, embarrassed.

'You had some difference of opinion between you?'

We both looked uncomfortable. 'We were not being the best of mates,' Sheila said.

'Children, children,' he said. 'Don't you know that when the redskins are on the prowl you're supposed to pull the wagons into a circle — not engage in sulks and personal disputes?'

'More to the point,' I said, anxious to change the subject, 'are you making any progress with tracking this loony down?'

'Not really,' he admitted. 'I have one good piece of news. I know who it wasn't.'

'It wasn't most of them,' said Sheila.

'It might have been,' he said. '*Murder on the Orient Express* — that's a murder by committee. So's *Service of All the Dead*.'

'Come on,' I said. 'Even Agatha Christie wouldn't stretch it as far as the descendants of six convicts from different places who happened by chance to be on the same ship all getting together to stop somebody writing a book about their ancestors!'

'Doesn't have to be all of them, boyo — just some.'

'Are you serious? Why, for heaven's sake?'

'A group of several members of the same family might have a common interest in suppressing some piece of information about the family,' he suggested.

'Like what?' I said.

'Oh, I don't know, bach. Perhaps they're a dynasty of brain surgeons and they don't want the public to know that there's hereditary insanity in the family.'

'You cannot be serious,' exclaimed Sheila.

'Well, yes and no,' he said. 'I wasn't really serious about the brain surgeons bit, but I do seriously suggest that we may be looking for more than one person.'

'Is this your good news?' said Sheila. 'That there may be busloads of loonies out there armed with bombs and knives and God knows what?'

'No, actually. I was sort of distracted by the possibilities. What I had been about to say was that it almost certainly isn't Mad Jack Garton.'

He unzipped his document case and pulled out a sheaf of photocopies, spreading them on the table.

'If,' he said, 'you read decent working-class newspapers, instead of the trendy liberal rubbish with which you waste your time, you would have known that Mad Jack's black ancestry has been well canvassed in the tabloids.'

From across two of the sheets a solid black headline announced, 'SEND 'EM HOME JACK HAS BLACK BLOOD'. Underneath, a photo of John Garton speaking at a rally was flanked by a reproduction of a painting. The caption read, 'Left, Mad Jack Garton speaks at an anti-refugee rally; Right, a portrait of his beautiful, pipe-smoking black ancestress which hangs in the Burton Gallery.'

I skimmed through the stories. There were five of them, all dating from about a year ago.

All five were similarly jeering in tone, but only the first one had the painting, which turned out to be *Negress with a Pipe of Tobacco* by 'Unknown' and may not have been Mad Jack's forebear at all, merely some other black lady of the period.

'So it wasn't your mad Nazi,' commented Sheila.

'It still might have been,' I said. 'He might have some other reason that we don't know about.'

'True,' said John, 'but that only puts him on a par with all the rest of the survivors of the six families, doesn't it?'

'So, you've managed to possibly eliminate one suspect,' I said. 'Well done!'

From the big Welshman's expression I expected a hot retort, but just then one of his team emerged from the back door to announce that they had finished photographing, fingerprinting and forensicking the kitchen. John asked him to send the bombs man out.

The bombs man was a scholarly bespectacled little plainclothes officer, with a beaming smile.

'Are you far enough finished to accept a glass of Mr Tyroll's excellent whisky?' John asked him.

'Oh, indeed,' he said. 'That would be most

welcome, It's very dusty in there, but I think we've finished with the scene.' He looked at his watch. 'In time for you to cook lunch, too,' he said, smiling. 'Apart from the bottom of the sink, everything else is OK. A bit dusty, but working.'

'What was it?' asked John.

'It was a shallow cardboard box — the kind you buy photographic paper in. Inside it was a thin tin container filled with the charge. It was detonated by a pressure device that moved when the end of the package was opened.'

'And what was it intended to do?' I asked.

'Very much what it did do,' he said. 'To go off very noisily, with a short sharp blast effect, very much like a stun grenade.'

'Not to kill or injure?' I said.

'Well, I won't say that it wouldn't injure if you were close to it, or even kill if you were elderly or had a dodgy heart, but that doesn't seem to be the intention.'

He finished his drink and left us. Sheila was looking thoughtful.

'How,' she asked, 'did he know that I'd been to the police museum?'

'Could he be tapping our phone?' I asked.

'I doubt it,' John replied. 'That's not as easy as people think. Are you still splashing about on the Internet, Sheila?'

She nodded. 'But I had Alasdair check for cookies and wipe them. So far as I know, no one can track where I've been and, anyway, I didn't deal with the museum through the Internet. I just phoned them.'

'Then he must be watching you, as we thought.'

'But even if he is — and I can't see how he is — how the blazes did he know that I had ordered photographs from the museum?'

'He knows what you're researching. We know he's been along the same trails himself. Presumably he's been to the museum and seen those photographs. He'd have known you'd want copies.'

'This is all getting to me,' she said and shuddered. She got up and walked into the house.

'You,' said John, 'were just about to sound off earlier on. You were just about to give me the old outraged public routine about 'Why aren't the police doing anything to stop this?', were you not?'

I nodded shamefacedly. 'Yes, John, I was, and I'm sorry, but you must see it from our point of view.'

'I do, boyo, I do. I wouldn't like this situation one little bit, even if you weren't friends. It's all very well to say that the package wasn't meant to kill or injure, but it could have done. He may not particularly want to kill, but he doesn't seem to care very much if it happens by accident as it were.'

'So what else is there to do?' I asked.

'Nothing, boyo, except be damned careful — all the time. Watch out for Sheila, watch out for yourself. Don't make unnecessary journeys. Keep this place secure. You know all this.'

'Secure?' I said. 'What's the point of keeping this place secure and not going out if the swine's simply going to send us exploding parcels? What'll the next one be — a jolly little packet of napalm?'

'No,' he said. 'I think he'll give up the letter-bomb trick now. He must know we're on to that. He won't expect you or Sheila to open anything yourselves now.'

'So, what's next?'

'I don't know, and that's what's worrying me. He ups the ante every time. From a stolen briefcase to a dead cat to a nasty psychological trick with a spider to an incendiary bomb to a stun bomb. What's his next step up?'

'I can't help feeling it might be a real honest-to-goodness bomb.'

He shook his head. 'No, I'm sure he'll stop that. He'll go off on a different tack — one we're not expecting.'

'Like what? Arsenic? Drive-by machine-gunning? Come on, John!'

He sighed. 'I'd like to nail him before his next move.'

'But you can't. What do we know about him? Nothing. We haven't a clue as to who he is or where he is or what it's really about.'

'We know he watches you — or someone watches you for him.'

'And what good is that?'

'Well,' he said, 'I have put a plain-clothes bloke on prowling about this area seeing who's moving and when, what's usual and what isn't, you know.'

'And what have you got?'

'Nothing much. It's a quiet street. During the day it's your neighbours going about their business, people visiting them — legitimately so far as we can tell. In the evening it's very similar, apart from the occasional incursion along the gully by teenage drunks and old whatsisname walking his dog. Nothing that looks out of order.'

'So how's he doing it, John? How the hell did he know about Sheila and spiders? Even I didn't know that! She's never told anyone in Britain.'

He had no answers. After he'd gone I called Mrs Dunk and asked her to set the kitchen to rights, and got a man in to fit a new sink. In the evening Sheila and I tried watching TV. Talking to each other was a strain. All our ears were still ringing and we got tired of conversing in a slow shout. TV that we couldn't hear properly wasn't much better, so we turned in early.

For the first time in days Sheila snuggled up against me in bed.

'I'm sorry,' she said.

'What about?'

'About the whole stupid thing, but most of all about going to market on you the other day. You didn't deserve it. It's just that — well, it's like the spiders thing — I like to know I can deal with things and it makes me angry when I can't, but I shouldn't have given you a blue. It's not your fault. If it's anybody's fault it's mine.'

'Don't be daft,' I said. 'It's not your fault some steaming psychopath takes exception to what you're doing.'

'Do you really want me to stop?' she asked.

'Of course not. I want you to be able to do whatever you want to do — safely. Anyway, as we've said before, stopping won't necessarily stop Jack the Cat-Ripper.'

'Anyway,' she said, 'I'm sorry.'

'So am I.'

'You don't have to say you're sorry.'

'I just did.'

'If you keep saying you're sorry I'll tear off your clothes and fall on you.'

'In that case, I'm very, very sorry — and anyway, I'm not wearing any clothes.'

22

After that we treated all mail with extreme caution. If we couldn't see through it by holding it up to the light, or if it felt a bit thick, or if we had any suspicions at all it was up to John Parry's man to suss it out. The day after the bomb came one of the maniac's cards:

RULE BRITANNIA,
MARMALADE AND JAM,
FIVE CHINESE CRACKERS
UP YOUR BACKSIDE,
BANG! BANG! BANG! BANG! BANG!

Inevitably it made us wonder if there were three more bombs on the way.

There was also, a day or two later, another package from the museum. That was examined by John's expert and pronounced clean. Sheila took one look at the contents and shrieked with delight, then carried them off to the study and hunched over them like a miser with a bag of sovereigns for an hour.

'Come on,' I said, when at last I managed to call her to the dinner table. 'Show and tell!'

She shook her head. 'Not till after dinner,' she said.

When food was over and the table cleared, she brought the museum packet and a file of papers to the table.

First she laid down a photocopy of a convict file.

'That's Jack Sullivan's particulars,' she said.

JACK SULLIVAN No 8714
tried 10th July 1865,
arrived Fremantle Barracks March 1866.
Born 3rd March 1849

Trade: None	Height: 5 ft. 6 in.
Complexn: Fair	Head: Round
Hair: Red	Whiskers: Moustache
Visage: Round & freckled	Forehead: M.Ht
	Eyes: Blue
Eyebrows: Red	Mouth: Wide
Nose: Wide	Remarks: Lateral
Chin: Rounded	scars on left ribs.
	Tattoo on l.upper
	arm — harp,
	shamrock and ERIN
	GO BRAGH.

Convict 7 years' transportation
Tried at Warwick, transported for assaults
Character: Violent

The summary of his convict career bore out the estimate of his character. Jack Sullivan had hardly passed a month in the barracks without attracting punishment. There were confinements, beatings and extra labour, running for pages, and always for assaults, on staff or fellow convicts. He had been released twice on a ticket-of-leave and recalled for fighting.

'A pretty hard doer, eh?' said Sheila, when I looked up.

'If that means what I think it does, yes — a pretty hard doer. A bloke who talked with his fists.'

'Seems like the whole family were much the same,' she said. 'Here, have a squid at this.'

She passed me a family tree of the Sullivans which she had drawn. 'It might help you to understand the pictures,' she said.

As I looked over the chart she slid a picture out of the packet. It was of a thickset fair man with heavy whiskers. From under a billycock hat he scowled at the camera.

'That', she announced, 'is young Jack's dad — Patrick Sullivan. He was photographed in 1861, when he was arrested for brawling in a pub. He was thirty-seven — middle-aged in those days — and he had convictions for fighting year in and year out. He'd done umpteen short sentences. Apparently when he wasn't in the cells he was a navvy.'

She laid down another picture. This time it was a younger version of the navvy — an equally surly youth in his teens.

'That', she said, 'is Jack's elder brother, Patrick. Sixteen when the picture was taken. Nicked for fighting. There's two more of him, as he grew up. In the last one he's twenty-four — still bashing people.'

I looked at the chart. 'What became of him?' I asked. 'There's no date of death.'

'Bit of a mystery,' she said. 'There's a scribble on the last picture which may say that he emigrated, but you can't read it properly. I can't find a death record that's definitely him, but there's no conviction after 1869.'

Another picture emerged — a fresh-faced teenager, but still with the family scowl. 'That's Connor,' she said. 'He hadn't got into the family trade. He's twelve there and about to go to a reformatory for stealing.'

'He died young,' I remarked, looking at the chart.

She nodded. 'Connor and his sister Catherine. He was thirteen, she was eleven. The death record says 'fever'. They died within two days of each other.'

I thought about what the slums of Brum

must have been like a hundred and fifty years ago. 'Typhoid? Scarlet fever? Cholera?' I asked.

'I don't know. The record just says 'fever'. I suppose the docs were overworked and weren't too particular about slum kids.'

' 'She died of a fever and no one could save her,' ' I quoted.

She pulled out three pictures together and hugged them to her chest before laying them down in a row.

'They're the jewels,' she announced. 'Those pictures are my JS. Young Jack before he got forcibly emigrated.'

Three pictures of a boy at about twelve, fourteen and seventeen.

'What was he into then?' I asked. 'Bashing people?'

'Not entirely. He started off where his brother Connor left off — stealing anything — but he took to his father's trade and ended up getting shipped out for assaults.'

'Surely they must have been pretty bad to warrant transportation? I mean, his dad never got transported.'

'I don't think it was what he did, so much as who he did it to. He was having one of his rare intervals of working at the building trade and I believe he thumped his boss and the boss's wife.'

'The boss's wife! If it had been his own wife they wouldn't have bothered. It would have been 'lawful correction'. How'd he come to bash the gaffer's wife?'

'I don't know yet,' she said. 'I think there's a bit of scandal in it. I reckon he was having an affair with the boss's lady and it all went wrong. If you thump a husband and wife it's more like a family blue than a public brawl.'

'You've got an overheated imagination,' I said. 'He might have had any kind of a row with his gaffer and the wife weighed in and got bashed.'

'Look at him,' she said. 'Sexy little devil at seventeen.'

I looked again. 'It must be the freckles,' I suggested. 'It's well known that people with freckles are sex-mad.'

'Only if they come across the right subject,' she scowled from behind her own mask of freckles. 'And they're getting very rare.'

'You've got the scowl!' I said. 'You haven't got Sullivan blood, have you? You're not the secret descendant of the missing Patrick? It'd explain a lot. Like your appetite for alcohol and your penchant for violence.'

'Get on!' she commanded, and laid down another photograph. Again the family resemblance showed in a man in his twenties.

'That's Eamon Daley,' she said. 'Jack's nephew.'

'He died young,' I remarked after a glance at the chart. 'He was only twenty-five or so. What killed him?'

'The law,' she said. 'Eamon was hanged at Warwick in 1891 for murdering a game-keeper.'

'He was a poacher?' I said.

'Not really,' she said. 'He was a brawler like the previous generation. By the time he shotgunned a gamekeeper he'd done lots of time for hitting people That's why they didn't believe him that it was self-defence.'

'Killing gamekeepers wasn't self-defence in those days,' I said. 'Poachers were assaulting the sacred rights of property. Don't forget — they used to get transported just for taking rabbits. Quite a lot of poachers got killed too, but that was all right — they were generally held to have deserved it.'

I looked at the diagram. 'His sister Mary died young,' I remarked. 'What was that? Slum fever again?'

'No,' she said. 'It was an accident. She was crushed by a cartwheel while playing in the streets. The Sullivans were an unlucky family.'

'Anyone who had to live in the slums of Victorian Brum must have been unlucky,' I said. 'It didn't need a penchant for drink and violence as well. Who's this Catherine Daley who stayed single? That's unusual, and she died fairly young. She didn't even make sixty.'

'She did well to make fifty-eight. Look at this!'

She slid out another trio of pictures. This time they were of a girl, at about fourteen and eighteen, and the same girl as a woman of about thirty-five. In every photograph she was over-painted and over-dressed in a cheap, flashy style.

'She was on the game!' I said.

'Too right. She's got pages and pages of convictions for soliciting.'

'And she had no kids?'

'I don't suppose she wanted them.'

'Maybe not, but contraception wasn't the order of the day for Victorian whores. She'd have had them whether she wanted them or not. But there's none registered to her?'

She shook her head.

'She might have had an unregistered one,' I speculated. 'Or more than one. There's never been any way to enforce registration of births and there wasn't the bureaucracy of the Welfare State then.'

'There's none shown with her in the censuses,' Sheila said. 'So perhaps she was lucky.'

'Either that,' I said, 'or there's some rich,

powerful bloke around who doesn't want you to reveal that his great-great-granny was a whore in Brum.'

'Do you really think so?'

'It's a possibility,' I said. 'It's not much worse than any of the others we've thought about. Better than John's dynasty of mad brain surgeons.'

'Can't be,' she said, firmly. 'If I can't find any offspring, her descendants wouldn't know who they are. Or, if for some reason they do know that they're descended from Ginger Kate — '

'Ginger Kate?' I interrupted.

'That's one of her trade names. Along with Red Kate and the Irish Cat. Don't interrupt. I was saying that, if her descendants did know who they were they would also know that I couldn't prove it. So it's not the Vengeance of Red Kate.'

'What about Patrick?' Her brother?' I asked.

'Ah, well, here we have the dawning of a different breed. Patrick Daley does not appear in the museum's records. He was never convicted of anything. He married Eileen Joyce and led a quiet life as a carpenter.'

'His kids seem to have been just as unlucky as his forebears, though,' I said. 'According to your chart, his eldest son Patrick died at nineteen, his second son Eamon at thirty-one and their sister Eileen at twenty-five. Only one of them — Mary — survived to raise a family.'

'I told you that this family of Daleys were a different breed. Patrick fought and died in South Africa and Eamon died in the Great War.'

'And what about Eileen?'

'Ah, yes, well, apparently the old traditions broke through in her case. She took after her Aunty Kate and went on the game in Brum.'

I laughed. 'Not so much the Old Adam as the Old Eve,' I said. 'So Pat and Eamon managed to sublimate their violent ancestral urges in fighting for their country, but Eileen got swept away on the lusts of the Sullivans.'

'Not so much of the sexism!' she complained. 'It was the only way an uneducated single woman could make a living in those days.'

She produced two more pictures. One was Eileen Joyce at seventeen. Like her Aunty Kate, over-dressed and over-painted, but beneath it all a really attractive young woman. The other showed a thinner, harder-faced woman, whose make-up was even heavier, presumably to cover the ravages of time or disease.

'What did she die of?' I asked.

'The record says 'consumption'.'

'Tuberculosis,' I said. 'Another of the delights of slum life. But her younger sister married?'

'Yes. She married another Joyce.'

'A relative?'

'I think he was a cousin. I'm checking into it. But neither of their kids survived. Patrick died when he was two — of 'fever' again. Eileen took to her aunty's trade — it seems to have run in the female side of the family — and only lived to be twenty-seven. I've got a picture of her when she was sixteen.'

She showed it, another pretty but over-blown girl.

'And what killed her at twenty-seven?'

'She did — she committed suicide.'

I shook my head at this long story of transportation and murder, disease and accident, crime and vice. 'Poor lass,' I said. 'They really were unlucky, weren't they, she Sullivan-Joyces?'

'Not as unlucky as the Daleys. Have a look at that branch at bottom right. That's Francis's family, descended from my Jack's nephew.'

'My God! What happened to them? They all died in the same year. What was it?'

'The luck of the Sullivans,' she said. 'They

decided to emigrate and they booked steerage tickets from Liverpool, but there was a coal strike on, so their bookings were changed. They were swapped to Southampton.'

Southampton? 1912? The light broke. 'The *Titanic*?' I asked.

She nodded. 'The whole family.'

'About two-thirds of the Irish immigrants on the *Titanic* died,' I said. 'If their bodies were recovered they'll be buried in Halifax, Nova Scotia.'

'Didn't they recover them all?' she said.

'No. Less than a third. For months after the Atlantic liners used to avoid the area of the sinking in case their passengers spotted corpses. Why are we talking about this?'

'Well,' she said, cheerfully, 'if you look on the bright side, it's great stuff for the book. Not just transportation, but murder, suicide, vice, even the *Titanic*.'

'You hard-hearted, mercenary wench!' I exclaimed.

'A poor girl still has to struggle to make a living on her own, kind sir, just like Red Kate and her niece.'

'No you don't,' I said, 'I'll make an honest woman of you whenever you want. Then you can share my genteel poverty.'

'Huh!' she snorted. 'If you'd have been alive in those days you'd have been defending the Sullivans and the Daleys and losing your cases and not getting paid.'

'Not fair,' I complained. 'I win quite a lot of cases. Bearing in mind that I start off with a disadvantage — a lot of my clients are actually guilty.'

'Yair, but you don't get paid very much.'

'I didn't think you wanted me for my money.'

'Just as well,' she said. 'Before we get hitched someone's got to produce some rhino round here, and it looks like it'll have to be me. Anyway, there's another good thing about the Sullivan-Daley-Joyces.'

'What's that?'

'They're all gone. They haven't left any descendants to sneak around cat-murdering and sending bombs through the mail.'

'No. I suppose not. Unless Patrick up the top of the chart there had kids.'

'I told you — he emigrated.'

'No. You told me that you thought he'd emigrated. Not clear evidence.'

'Oh, come, Chris Tyroll! Next you'll be saying that little Eamon Daley sank the *Titanic* by pulling the plug out and the descendants don't want anyone to find out!'

'One day remind me to tell you about the bloke who embezzled his company's cash and booked on the *Titanic*. They never found his body after the sinking, but they never found anyone who saw him on board, either. Having been listed missing was the best thing that ever happened to him. I don't suppose his descendants are very keen on owning up!'

'Rubbish! You're not suggesting that Francis's mob survived and are still around?'

'No, not really, but Patrick the emigrant's might be.'

23

We tried to follow John Parry's advice. Sheila stuck to her computer, sometimes striving to track down the last of her six targets, sometimes drafting sections of her book. In the evenings we locked up and stayed in.

Most days I still had to be in my office or in a court, and I disliked leaving Sheila alone at home, but there seemed no other solution. I suggested to her that she might work on one of the office computer terminals during the day, but she pointed out that our loony would soon catch on and make a target of the office. That seemed reasonable, but I was still unhappy with the alternative. I was always relieved to arrive home and find her present and unharmed.

Claude dropped in to the office one afternoon and announced that he had some results for Sheila. He would have passed them on to me, but I had the feeling that she would never have forgiven either of us for depriving her of the pleasure so I invited him to eat with us and present his report.

Sheila let him get as far as the dessert before she started pestering him. He took out a pocket notebook and laid it by his plate.

'I had another job in Shropshire,' he said, 'with a fair amount of time to waste, so I went across to the village and hung about the village pub. Once we'd established that I wasn't a plainclothes licensing nark, we all got along famously.'

He stopped and attacked his dessert again.

'Well, come on!' Sheila urged.

'They don't like Bradley much in the Crown and Cushion. They think he's some kind of nutter. I heard all about how his wife left him — '

'He had a wife?' Sheila interrupted.

'Yes, he did. Apparently she left him a few years ago.'

'Why?' Sheila demanded.

Claude took another leisurely spoonful and savoured it.

'Well,' he said at last, 'I heard all sorts of reasons. Some said it was drink, but the landlord said he never set foot in the pub and the postman said he never saw empty bottles in the rubbish bin. Some thought she just left him because he was 'crazy'.'

'What kind of crazy?' I asked.

'I asked that. One bloke thought he was 'music-crazy', that he'd gone bonkers through pounding the piano. He said, 'Any time you went past there — day or night — he was hammering away at the joanna. 'Tisn't natural, that. I likes a bit of a tune as well as the next, but you dunna want it all the blooming time.' '

'You can discount that,' I said. 'That's just the English suspicion of art. They don't like education very much, so they wouldn't have cared for a schoolteacher anyhow, but there's nothing upsets the English like painting or writing or playing an instrument. They think they're all deeply un-English ways of going on. How else did they say he was crazy?'

'The postman said that he called at the farm one morning and Bradley was in the garden — dancing.'

'Dancing?' Sheila and I said simultaneously.

'Dancing is what the man said. He told me that Bradley was twisting about in the garden. He called to him, but Bradley took no notice of him, so he pushed the mail through the door and went about his business.'

'Now there's a deeply suspicious going-on,' I said. 'Dancing in your own garden. I'm surprised it isn't a crime.'

'Shut up and let Claude get on!' commanded Sheila.

Claude had finished his dessert, so he wound Sheila up a bit further, by carefully consulting his notebook.

'The generality of opinion,' he said, at last, 'was that it was either drink or child abuse that sent his wife off.'

'So they had children?' Sheila pounced.

'A child. One son.'

'When were they married?' I asked.

'In the mid-1980s. The boy was born soon after.'

'There you are,' said Sheila, triumphantly. 'A wife and a young boy. The photos you saw. But I still can't understand why I couldn't find the marriage record.'

'Probably because it wasn't in Britain,' said Claude. 'He married her abroad. Majority of opinion said she was German. A few more discerning types reckoned she was Dutch or Scandinavian.'

'What about the child abuse?' I asked. 'Do you reckon there's anything in that?'

'I doubt it,' he said. 'It seems that whenever anyone called there the lad was playing the piano, but that was so whether his father was there or not. Maybe he did it because he liked it. Apparently he was pretty good at it. They said he'd played at a couple of concerts for the village church. The first time they thought they were in for a boring session of classical music, but he surprised them with ragtime and boogie as well as classics. That's about all I could find out from the pub — that

Bradley's crazy, that his boy's a talented pianist, that his wife's some kind of foreigner and that she left him and took the boy either through drink or child abuse.'

'Not drink,' I said.

'Why not?' asked Claude. 'I know he didn't use the local, but a lot of alcoholics don't. They're too ashamed. They get their booze elsewhere and drink at home.'

'Sure,' I said, 'but I get to meet a lot of alkies in my trade and he just didn't come across as one. His house was cold and dusty, but it didn't seem like an alky's lair. What do you think, Sheila? You were in his kitchen, that ought to give him away.'

She thought and shook her head slowly. 'No,' she said. 'I'm with you, Chris. Whatever he is, he isn't a lush. The kitchen was probably just like his wife left it when she shot through. He's one of those guys who uses one cup and one plate each day and lives on cans and the microwave, but it didn't look like a boozer's kitchen.'

'Did you get anything else?' I asked Claude.

He smiled. 'Thought you'd never ask,' he said. 'I know what the wife says about it all.'

'How?' Again Sheila and I were simultaneous.

'Because I've chatted to her, that's how.'

238

'I told you he's the best,' I said to Sheila. 'Come on, tell all.'

'Well,' he said, 'after getting all I could out of the guys in the Crown and Cushion, it occurred to me that the postman seemed a pretty alert sort of bloke — '

'You mean nosy,' Sheila interrupted.

'Well, yes, that as well. Anyway, I let on to him — in deepest confidence, you understand — that I was instructed by a solicitor who might have good news for Mrs Bradley if she could be traced. He huffed and puffed a bit about being a servant of the Crown and he was a bit suspicious that I might be up to something on the husband's behalf.'

'So what happened?' Sheila asked.

'I was able to assure him that I was not acting for Mr Bradley and, as to his being a servant of the Crown, well, those instructing me were prepared to make reasonable payments for information, but if he felt unable to accept I would quite understand. So we reached an agreement, money changed hands and he told me that she was living in Telford under her maiden name.'

'How does he know that?' I asked.

'Because she still writes to Bradley and, as he put it, 'puts her name and address on the back, the way they do abroad because their post isn't very reliable'.'

When we'd had our laugh he looked at the notebook and went on. 'The former Mrs Bradley now calls herself Anna van Rijs and I've got an address here for her in Telford.'

'But you said you'd talked to her,' Sheila said.

'So I did, and I was coming to that, but I thought it was coffee time.'

Sheila scowled. 'If you open your mouth while I'm making the coffee, I'll brain you, Claude,' she threatened, and stalked off to the kitchen. She was back in no time at all.

'It's instant,' she announced, and poured. 'Now, where were you?'

'I was about to explain how, by an ingenious ruse, I gained the confidence of Mrs Bradley and got into conversation with her.'

He sipped his coffee. 'Delicious,' he said. 'It was coffee that was the clue. I got the impression that the postman had a soft spot for the lady. It seems she used to take pity on him when her husband was at work — no, not that kind of pity! — she used to invite him in for a mug of coffee. So I thought I'll try the same trick.'

'You disguised yourself as the postman?' I said.

'No, no. I waited for a really sweltering hot afternoon and called at her door as a market researcher. It worked like a charm. She took pity on this poor, sweaty bloke on her doorstep and invited me in for a cool drink. Once across the doorstep it was a piece of cake.'

'So what did she say?' demanded Sheila.

'She told me about her husband, how he'd taken to drinking in secret — '

'If it was in secret, how'd she know?' I interrupted, because I still didn't see Ian Bradley as a drinker.

'She said he used to fall about and slur his words. She didn't mind that so much — she thought he was under stress at work and that he was taking a few before he came home — but then he started getting jumpy and bad-tempered and taking it out on her and the boy.'

'Did you see the boy?' Sheila asked.

'No. He was at school, but she showed me his picture. It must have been the same one that you saw, Chris, the one sitting at a piano.'

'You really chummed up with her, didn't you?' I remarked, and perhaps it sounded more sarcastic than I intended it to be.

Claude looked at me wide-eyed. 'I assure you', he said, 'that at all times I kept the ethics of my profession well in mind.'

'Oh yes,' I said. 'Bribing postmen to break

confidences and misleading a woman on her own!' I was beginning to feel guilty about the whole Bradley episode. I couldn't escape the feeling that Sheila had launched on an unwarranted invasion of Bradley's life.

'Shut up, Chris!' commanded Sheila. 'Whose side are you on? Tell us about the boy, Claude.'

'Well, she's very proud of her son, and with good reason, it seems.'

He reached into the inside pocket of his jacket and pulled out a couple of pages of photocopies.

'Look at those,' he said, laying them on the table.

They were copies of news stories and one carried the photograph of the boy pianist I had seen in Bradley's home. They recorded the fact that fourteen-year-old Graham van Rijs had won the Midlands heat of a national musical competition and that he had gone on to win a place in the national final.

'So he takes after his father,' Sheila commented. 'That must be the one talented kid he told us about.'

'Perhaps that's what the trouble was all about,' I suggested.

They both looked at me questioningly.

'Bradley wanted a career as a musician, but decided he wasn't good enough to make the big time,' I said. 'Then he discovered that his son had a superior talent and that he himself had arthritis and couldn't even play. So, while his son was starting to win acclaim, he had lost the ability to play at all. Perhaps his bad temper was jealousy and frustration.'

'Could be,' Sheila agreed.

I went to the sideboard and poured myself a large whisky.

'I don't really like any of this,' I said. 'Bradley's a lonely, frustrated bloke who's had enough dumped on him. His wife has had to make hard decisions and his kid's just starting out on what might be a great career. I'm not at all sure you ought to be poking about in their affairs, Sheila.'

'Maybe not,' she said. 'Though a juvenile musical genius would be good for the book. Anyway, it's early days to be deciding what should be in and what shouldn't.'

24

John Parry came around one evening to tell us the results of the scientific examination of the remains of the stun bomb.

'Nothing very special about it,' he said. 'As we said at the time, the cardboard box was a standard box for photographic paper, sold all over the world. The tin liner was cobbled together out of an old biscuit box, by someone with a minimal knowledge of metalwork.'

'What about the explosives?' I asked.

'Again, simple stuff. Routine ingredients you can buy in chemists and hardware stores if you know what you need. The trigger was a version of the one he used on the incendiary bomb — a pressure button that would move once you released the wrappings — so it's definitely from the same sender.'

'As if we doubted it,' I said.

'Have you found any more suspects for me?' he asked Sheila.

'Well, there's a very long shot,' she said, and outlined the sad saga of Jack Sullivan's family.

'Won't be them,' John said, shaking his head.

'You sound pretty sure,' I commented.

'Stands to reason, boyo. Our man, we reasonably believe, has been researching the same areas as Sheila and finding the same results.'

We both nodded.

'Right, then. If he's looking in the same places he's only got the same information, so he won't know what happened to Patrick Sullivan either.'

'Hold on a minute,' Sheila said. 'If he is — himself — a descendant of Patrick Sullivan, he will know that his branch of the family is still alive and well, won't he?'

'Yes,' said John, patiently, 'but he will also know that you don't know that. What's more, if he were a descendant of Patrick he'd have to be daft to draw attention to himself. He might be the cause of you catching on that his family still exists, mightn't he?'

'True,' she agreed. 'So we can rule that whole lot out as suspects.'

'What about your Staffordshire bloke?' John asked. 'Have you tracked him yet?'

'I'm pretty certain,' she said. 'Hang on, I'll get the papers.'

She disappeared and was back quickly with a folder.

'Look,' she said, laying papers on the table.

'This is Jim Simmonds' convict record.'
It was the now familiar format:

JAMES SIMMONDS No 7172
tried 18th July 1865,
arrived Fremantle Barracks March 1866.
Born 10th January 1845

Trade: Apprentice engraver

Complexn: Swarthy

Hair: Black curled

Visage: Narrow

Eyebrows: Black

Nose: Small

Chin: Rounded

Height: 5 ft. 6 in.

Head: Long

Whiskers: None

Forehead: High

Eyes: Black

Mouth: Wide

Remarks: Burn scars on both hands. No tattoos.

Convict 7 years' transportation

Tried at Stafford, transported for theft as servant

Character: Good

There was very little record of punishments. Jim Simmonds had been a model prisoner and had been released at the first opportunity.

'Description could be you,' John remarked

'I'm taller,' I said, 'but the character might be me.'

'What's 'theft as servant'?' Sheila asked.
'It says he was an apprentice. Surely

they weren't servants?'

'To all intents and purposes, they were,' I said. 'But 'theft as servant' merely means that whatever he stole belonged to his boss. It just meant stealing from an employer. They took a dim view of it, in fact the courts still do. It's treated as a breach of trust.'

'So what have you got on his family, Sheila?' John asked.

'Well,' she said, 'it didn't take me long to find out that he was the third and youngest son of John Simmonds and Martha Whitton of Stafford. I had been going to follow the Simmonds family down until I got that broadsheet ballad about Jim. That says he had a sweetheart and a son by her.'

'They were awful liars, broadsheet writers,' I said. 'Remember the one about Jack Smythe's hanging that never was.'

'Right,' she said. 'But I had to check it out, and there in the 1871 census is a Katherine Evans, daughter of Daniel Evans and Bronwen Morgan, living in Great Wyrley.'

She pronounced it 'Great Wirely'.

'It's Great Wurley,' I said. 'Evans and his wife must have come up to the Staffordshire coalfield from Wales.'

'Right again,' she said. 'Evans is described as a miner and his place of birth and his wife's is in South Wales.'

'But how can you tell that this Katherine Evans is the Kate Evans in the song?' I asked. 'It's not an uncommon name.'

'No, but the census shows a five-year-old boy sharing the Evans family home and he is listed as 'James Simmonds'. Am I right or am I right?'

'It certainly looks as if you're right,' I agreed. 'So what then?'

'That's when things turned a bit difficult. I thought I'd solved the awkward bit, but I hadn't. I couldn't find Kate Evans or little Jimmy Simmonds in the next census.'

'She'd left the area?' John suggested.

'That's what I thought at first. I had visions of trawling through marriage records at the Family Centre and never finding her because she hadn't married or she'd emigrated or something, but then I found her again. She had married. To a bloke called Thomas Lewis, another miner. What confused me was that in the 1881 survey there's no fifteen-year-old James Simmonds.'

'He'd died?' I asked.

'No. He was alive and well, but living under a new name. Kate married Thomas Lewis in 1873 and they had four children — Thomas, David, Bronwen and Alan — but the census showed them with another child, James Lewis aged fifteen.'

'So, Lewis had done the decent thing and given Jim's child his name,' I said.

'That must be the answer,' she said.

'And then what?' I asked.

'James Lewis married in 1888 to a Jennifer Wilde, and they had four kids — Thomas, Katherine, Richard and John. Thomas was a miner, Katherine married a miner, Richard died as an infant and John stayed a bachelor.'

'What about Thomas?' John asked.

'He produced three offspring — John, Thomas and Elizabeth — and his sister Kate had four — Daniel, Luke, Mark and Katherine.'

'So, we've got two lines of direct descent from your Jim Simmonds and proliferating offspring,' remarked John.

Sheila nodded. 'Right,' she agreed. 'Now John Lewis, the bachelor, you can ignore if you like. He ended up in a funny farm.'

'An asylum?' I said.

'Right. He was born in 1892 and was locked up in 1928.'

'Maybe we can't ignore him,' said John. 'What was his trouble? Do you know?'

'The death record says 'General paresis of the insane'. What's that?'

'Syphilitic insanity,' I said.

Sheila went on. 'John, Thomas and Elizabeth Lewis all married. John's marriage was childless, luckily for us — and for the family. He was another who was certified, in 1942. Thomas Lewis had two kids — Katherine and Elizabeth — and his sister Elizabeth Lewis had three — Richard, John and Mary.'

'Hang on a minute,' I said. 'We're well into this century by now, and there's the cousins — Daniel Lewis and that lot — there must be masses of them around now.'

'There are,' she said, glumly. 'What's more, most of them are called Jones. They're scattered all over Staffordshire and the West Midlands. Look!'

She produced a family tree with addresses jotted on it.

'You're not going to interview all these, are you?' I asked.

'Not unless I have to,' she said and laid down another paper. 'That's a simplified version,' she said. 'I thought I might start with that lady,' and she pointed to a name.

'Katherine, born 1934,' I read 'She never married?'

'Right. She's still alive, and I'm hoping she'll have been maiden aunty to the whole clan for decades. If so, she can tell me anything that anyone else can, and probably lots that the others can't.'

'Sounds better than going through the

whole extended clan,' I said. 'What do you reckon John?'

'I reckon that I shall have to check the whole lot out for criminal tendencies,' he said, gloomily. 'Let us have a list of full names, dates of birth and addresses will you, Sheila, and I'll run them on the computer. What about your other dead end — John Lewis, the one who was certified?'

'What about him?'

'What was his problem?'

'Schizophrenia.'

'Isn't that hereditary?' I asked.

'They're still arguing about that one,' John said. 'Still, two of them certified in two successive generations is strange.'

'Different causes,' I observed

'If the shrinks were right,' he said. 'Have you ever known them right? I take it you haven't found any more maniacs in this tribe?'

'To be honest, I can't be sure. There's so many of the Jones branch that I haven't sorted them all out yet.'

'Wonderful,' he sighed. 'A tribe of homicidal nutters, all called Jones.'

25

You can't stay scared all the time. Well, at least, not full pitch, hysterical, trembling scared. You walk through snake country and at first you look about you carefully, but after a while you get distracted by other things.

Days passed and Jack the Cat-Ripper left us alone. We still stayed close to base, but I began to be a bit less wary. I imagine Sheila was the same. Sometimes I caught myself at it and reminded myself of what our man had already done and what he might yet do, but it doesn't work. You really cannot stay one hundred per cent alert all the time.

Evenings when we had no visitors we sat around and stared at television until we'd reminded ourselves how bad most of it is, then gave up. Sheila's discovery of my mother's record collection kept her endlessly amused. A lot of nights we sprawled on the sitting-room floor with a bottle of wine, while Frank Crumit or Billy Bennett or Bob Dylan or Cisco Houston warbled away on the stereo.

For the umpteenth time she asked me to remember when my mother and I met Bob

Dylan at the Newport Festival.

'I've told you,' I said. 'He was just some bloke at the time, and I was a toddler. Of course, if I'd only realised he was going to be an international superstar I'd have got myself photographed with him and had it autographed.'

'All right, all right! Don't get off your bike, I've just never met anyone who's met Bob Dylan before.'

'You might as well not have done now, since I can't remember a damn thing about him. I remember Woody Guthrie, though. We went to see him in hospital and he sang songs to me.'

'What did he do?'

'What did he do? Inspired Bob Dylan, that's what. What do you think 'Song to Woody' is about? He wrote about a thousand songs of which you probably know several, like 'This Land Is Your Land' or 'Grand Coulee Dam'.'

'What was he in hospital for? Booze or drugs?'

'What a cynic you are! He had a rare condition that killed him in the end. For years people thought he was drunk when he wasn't, but it didn't make much difference when they diagnosed it. It's always fatal. He died of it in his fifties.'

'Nasty,' she said and rolled over to shuffle through the record shelves. She slid out a Guthrie album and clambered up to put it on the player.

She was half-way across the room when the window exploded inwards. At the same time something whirred across the room and struck the furniture with a thud.

I grabbed Sheila's ankle and dragged her back down to the floor.

'What the hell was that?' she gasped.

'I don't know,' I said, 'but we know who. Lie there while I get the lights out.'

I reached up and switched off the table lamps that were the room's only lights. It was full dark outside and it took a little while for our eyes to get accustomed to the blackness. When they had I managed to find the phone and dial 999.

'What now?' Sheila hissed in my ear.

'Now we lie here, keep quiet and don't show any light or movement till the fuzz arrive.'

'What smashed the window? A bullet?'

'I don't think so. It was too slow, but it was pretty powerful, whatever it was.'

She raised her head and peered towards the window. 'He must be outside,' she said.

'If he's got any sense he'll be gone,' I said. 'He must know the police will be here soon.'

'But he might still be out there,' she persisted.

'He might,' I agreed. 'He might still be lurking in the shrubs at the far end, then when we look out of the window he'll have a marvellous target — two pale blobs inside a dark rectangle. Then he can whang whatever it was came through the window straight into your pretty face. Which I'd really rather he didn't do.'

'Good on you,' she said, 'but the swine will get away before the police get here. It's our best chance to nail him.'

'Since he hasn't tried again,' I said, 'I'm willing to bet that he's made off by now. Anyway — listen!'

Somewhere a dog was barking, but the distant honking of police sirens announced that two or more cars were on their way up the hill.

'He'll certainly be on his way now,' I said.

Within seconds we heard three police cars pulling up in front of the house. I switched the lights on again and opened the front door. A handful of uniformed officers led by a sergeant swarmed in, while others deployed around the garden.

Briefly I explained to the sergeant the nature of the attack.

'What was it, sir? You said you didn't think it was a bullet.'

'No, sergeant. I've been shot at before and it didn't sound like a bullet. It sounded slower and heavier, but whatever it was it took out the window at one go.'

I showed the sergeant the sitting-room, both of us standing at the open door so as not to disturb any evidence.

'You can see where the window broke from the pattern of the broken glass,' I said. 'Whatever it was went somewhere over there.' I pointed towards a bookcase. 'That suggests to me that he was either standing on the lawn to the right of the pond or in the shrubs by the back gate.'

The sergeant nodded. 'We'd better leave this room till the Scene of Crimes officer gets here. Is there somewhere else we can sit?'

I led him through to the kitchen and Sheila put the coffee pot on.

'DI Parry's on his way, sir,' said the sergeant. 'He's off duty, but there's a standing order in the Control Room that he's to be called in to any emergency involving this address or either of your names.'

He had hardly spoken when John ambled in from the front door. 'One large coffee, please, Sheila,' he said. 'Evening all, or is it morning?'

He dropped into a chair at the table. He was wearing a grey tracksuit, a garment that he only adopted when scrambling out of bed in the middle of the night.

'Hello, John. We got you up,' I remarked.

He nodded. 'The Scene of Crime bloke's in your sitting-room,' he said. 'Tell me about it.'

Briefly I outlined what had happened.

'And you wanted to go after him?' he said to Sheila.

'Well, for the first time we could be sure that he was somewhere near. It seemed like a good chance to get our hands on him. Anyway, I've got a strong urge to defongerate the bastard.'

'De-fon-ger-ate,' John repeated, rolling each syllable around. He widened his eyes and sipped his coffee. 'Does it ever strike you, Chris, that she invents these colourful colonialisms to entertain us simple Brits?'

'For your information, you big Pommy plod, defongerate is a perfectly decent Aussie word. Our gardener used to use it when I was a kid.'

'Gardener!' he exclaimed. 'And I thought that — '

Sheila banged her coffee mug down so hard that the table shook. 'It may have escaped your notice, Inspector Parry,' she

257

said, 'but some crazy galah is out there trying to do me harm, and I had the silly and perhaps mistaken idea that you were trying to arrest him. Instead, you're sitting here swilling coffee and making snide Pommy jokes!'

'While I sit here swigging coffee,' he said, calmly, 'my officers are searching the area in the dark for the aforementioned crazy galah, notwithstanding his possession of an unknown but apparently dangerous weapon. My Scene of Crime officer is in your sitting-room, trying to develop clues that will help to identify our man, and two uniformed officers and a detective constable are annoying all your neighbours by knocking them up late and asking them if they know anything that will help. If you can think of anything I can usefully do apart from co-ordinating their efforts I shall gladly go away and do it.'

While he made this speech I had got up, fetched a bottle of brandy and topped up everyone's coffee — generously.

'I shouldn't,' he said. 'Not on duty.'

'You're not on duty,' I said. 'The sergeant told us.'

'Damno!' he exclaimed. 'That's the excuse I'd forgotten. I am not required to notice things when not on duty.'

Sheila, who had been pale with anger while she sounded off at John, was now blushing. She got up and flung her arms around him from the back.

'Sorry,' she said. 'I know you're doing your best.'

They were still in that pose when a plain-clothes detective walked in.

'Sorry, John,' he said. 'Should I have knocked?'

'Not at all,' said the big Welshman, quite unruffled. 'Dr McKenna was merely easing the strain in my shoulders. Have you got anything?'

The officer held out a plastic evidence bag. John took it, examined the contents and laid it on the table. 'Where was it?' he asked.

'It was embedded in the far end of a bookcase to the left of the fireplace. Stuck in about an inch.'

Sheila and I were both peering at the bag's content. It was a metal shaft, only a few inches long, with moulded fins around one end and a viciously sharp point at the other.

'A quarrel!' I exclaimed.

'A what?' said Sheila.

'A quarrel,' said John. 'A crossbow bolt.'

'I suppose in this antiquated country it's only reasonable that even the maniacs use medieval weapons,' she said.

John was turning the bag in his hands. The light kept catching the weapon's point, which had evidently been ground sharp.

'Don't mock,' he said. 'These things are as dangerous as a firearm. Your army used them in Vietnam and our army trained yours to use them. They used to go through armour in the old days.'

'A bit specialised, aren't they?' I said.

He shook his head. 'You can buy them by mail order if you know where to look. A longbow — like Robin Hood and the Welsh bowmen at Agincourt used — takes practice, but crossbows are much easier. They're like pistols, a little bit of practice and you can become reasonably accurate.'

'It's a big thing to sneak about with,' Sheila commented. 'If anybody saw him he'd be a bit stuck for an explanation, wouldn't he?'

'Probably used one of those little ones with a pistol grip,' he said. 'They're small enough to hide under a coat.'

'Is it any help?' I asked. 'In tracing him, I mean.'

'We can find out who made this bolt. It's obviously a commercial job, though someone's sharpened it up. I imagine that the same people who make the bows make the quarrels, so we might know who made his weapon and we just might be able to track where it was bought, but I wouldn't bet on it.'

He turned to his detective. 'Anything else?' he asked.

The man shook his head. 'Only the broken glass. That shows more or less where the window broke and gives a rough trajectory of the shot. I'd say he was in the far corner of the garden, towards the gate. I've told the lads to be careful and not go trampling all over it in the dark. We'll see things better in daylight.'

John nodded and pulled his phone from the pouch pocket on the belly of his tracksuit. He pressed buttons and spoke.

'Peter? Have you done yet? Right, come through to the kitchen when you get here.'

He switched off. 'That's my boy who's been watching this street. He's finished annoying your neighbours for the time being and he's coming in to report.'

Sheila poured more coffee and added another mug when another plain-clothes officer turned up.

'This is DC Harden,' John said. 'Anyone seen anything or heard anything?'

He shook his head. 'Very little,' he said. He took out a notebook and flipped through it. 'There's an old boy who lodges down on the far side — you know, sir, the one who walks his dog along here every night? I had high hopes of him, but he was in a state of meltdown. Seems he was in the road with Fido and heard the window go. He panicked — thought it was the hooligans who rough-housed him recently — and wanted to get home a bit smart, but Fido went barking crazy and tried to run off and catch himself a villain.'

'Pity he didn't get the chance,' Sheila remarked. 'I wouldn't have minded you identifying him by the pieces bitten off his bum!'

DC Harden grinned. 'No such luck,' he said. 'The old man tugged his pooch home and collapsed in his landlady's sitting-room.'

'What? Literally?' I asked.

'Well, no, not really. Fell into an armchair wheezing and panting and twitching. Scared witless, he was. She gave him so much booze he was nearly kali'd by the time we got to him. Still, at least he gave us the time.'

'And he was outside but he didn't see anyone come out of the gully?' John asked.

'No, that's what he was scared of.'

'Then our man must have gone along the lane between the garden and the brass-foundry,' I said.

'Where were you when it happened, Peter?' John asked.

'Up the other end, unfortunately, near the main road.'

The uniformed sergeant and one of his constables joined us. The constable was carrying a small sheet of cardboard with a coloured object laid on it.

'Inspector,' the Sergeant said, 'we've done the best we can in the dark. We've been carefully over the lawn with lamps and along the path, but we've left the area around the shrubs till daylight. We found this on the path, just in front of the gate.'

He took the sheet of cardboard from his constable and laid it on the table. On top of it lay a small circular tin, about three and a half inches in diameter. The lid was printed with a colourful design of two parrots, one with a biscuit in its beak, and the name 'McClones Water Biscuits'.

'Victorian repro,' I said. 'The old biscuit firms made these little tins to hold samples. Now they make cheap repros out East and you can buy them in fancy goods shops and discount stores.'

'Seen it before, either of you?' John asked.

'Not that one,' I said, and Sheila shook her head.

John looked carefully at the tin, then beckoned the Scene of Crime man to have a look. 'Any prints on it?' he asked.

'No, sir. It would take a print well on that shiny metal, but there's none there. Still, I'd have to dust it to be certain.'

John lifted the cardboard and weighed it in his hand. 'There's something in it,' he said. 'It's dry and clean so it mustn't have been there long. You two don't recognise it. I reckon our friend may have left us a clue at last.'

26

Then there was Sawney. It didn't make any difference that a psychopath armed with a medieval weapon was lurking in my shrubbery seeking to maim or kill the woman I loved — there was still Sawney, and his case was about to go into court.

I suppose I could have wriggled out of it. I could have told Alasdair that I was so traumatised by the attack on Sheila that I wasn't fit to appear in court. He'd have done it for me, but deep down I'd never have forgiven myself. Nor would Sawney. He expected personal service from me. So I gritted my teeth and ambled across the square to the Guildhall.

He was waiting for me on the steps. He wore a blazer with the badge of some athletic association which I'm sure he never graced and his thinning hair — which varied between bright red and deep auburn had settled for a medium ginger. No greeting, just a torrent of complaints as soon as I walked up.

'Do you know which court we're in? We're in Number One! That's Billingham's court, isn't it? I'm not going to be tried by him! He's tried me before. He'll be prejudiced.'

I tried suggesting that magistrates see an awful lot of defendants and they probably don't remember many of them.

'He'll remember me,' he declared. 'He threatened to sentence me for contempt.'

Major Billingham is a personification of all the traditional English virtues. I know this because he goes to some trouble to make it plain. In fact he was both stupid and bigoted. I know that because I know that he regarded me as a dangerous radical. Personally I sympathised with Sawney's desire not to be tried by the Major's Bench, but I wasn't sure we could get out of it.

'I'll speak to the usher,' I said.

'Batman' the usher — so-called because of the long black gown that he whipped about him as he strode around the lobby — button-holed me inside the door.

'Morning, Mr Tyroll. Here for Sawney, are you?' and he jotted a note on his clipboard.

'Yes,' I said, 'but there's a problem.'

'Problem?' he said. 'Problem? What problem's that, sir?'

'My client says that his case is listed before the Major's Bench.'

'That's right, sir. Number One.'

'Ah, well, you see he says that he's been up

in front of the Major before and says he was threatened with contempt.'

The usher stared at me from behind his horn-rimmed glasses for a long moment. Then the penny dropped.

'Is he suggesting that he won't get a fair trial in front of the Major, sir?' he said, as though the very idea was a sin against the Holy Ghost.

'Well,' I said, 'that's what he seems to think,' as though nothing was further from my own ideas.

Batman scanned his clipboard with a disapproving frown.

'Nothing can be done,' he announced at last. 'Number Two is taking only guilty pleas and yours is a trial. I can't shift it over. It'd upset everything.'

'What about an adjournment? If I ask for an adjournment, could we get it in front of someone else soon?'

He delved in the papers at the back of his clipboard and a smile dawned.

'We could indeed, sir. If it went over till Wednesday, we've got an extra court sitting Wednesday. The chairman will be Mr Birtle.'

'I thought he'd retired.'

'He did, sir, but he's still commissioned and he sits now and then when we're busy.'

Birtle was a cadaverous old clown who was

both stupid and rude. If there was a worse choice than Billingham it was Birtle.

'I'll speak to my client,' I said. 'I'm sure we can sort something out.'

Sawney was by the tea and coffee machine. 'Have you changed it?' he demanded.

I poked cash in the machine and drew myself a lemon tea. I smiled at him. 'There's no problem,' I said. 'We can get your case adjourned till Wednesday.'

He looked suspicious. 'They don't normally take trials on Wednesdays,' he said. 'Who's the chairman on Wednesday?'

'I don't know,' I lied. 'But it won't be Major Billingham. Ask the usher.'

Sawney strode across the lobby and accosted Batman. Seconds later he was back, looking pale and stunned.

'They've brought Birtle out on Wednesday!' he exclaimed. 'I'm not going in front of him! He committed me to Crown Court for sentence last time. Said I was a hardened offender who needed a lesson. I'm not going in front of him!'

'So what do we do?' I asked.

'It's all right,' he said. 'I've told the usher I'll be tried today.'

While he got himself another drink I settled down on a bench and smiled to myself behind my *Independent*. At least I'd won the

268

first round. Then I stopped smiling — I'd still got the Major to contend with.

Sawney's case was called after an hour or so. Once in the courtroom I could see that it wasn't just Billingham I'd have to contend with. His two colleagues were an over-painted lady with a wide hat, whose name I have never known, and a little man in a blue suit who has sat for twelve years and never, to my knowledge, said a word.

Sawney's co-accused had already pleaded guilty and her case had been adjourned to await the outcome of Sawney's trial. If he got convicted her advocate would be able to say that it was all Sawney's fault, that he led her astray. She would get less and Sawney would get more.

The Crown Prosecutor launched his evidence. I didn't have a great deal to do at first, because there wasn't anything I could do. We couldn't deny that the radio/cassette was stolen, nor who it was stolen from, nor that it fetched up with the girl, so the first few witnesses passed quickly. Then we got to Sawney's arrest and arrival at the police station. The first of the two arresting officers was in the witness box. According to him it had all gone like clockwork. Once in custody, Sawney had freely admitted his part in the crime and made a voluntary statement, which he now produced.

I rose to cross-examine.

'Sergeant, when you and PC Allen first spoke to Mr Sawney and made him aware of the nature of your enquiry, what did he say to you?'

'He said, 'She's a liar. I don't know anything about it.' '

'And that was after PC Allen cautioned him, so that remark is evidence, is it not?'

'Yes, sir.'

'Thank you. Now, you took him to the police station and put him in front of the custody sergeant. I'm sure you know that it is one of the custody sergeant's duties to ensure that a proposed detainee is fit to be held in custody?'

'Yes, sir.'

'And was my client fit — in your opinion?'

'He'd been shaking a bit in the car, sir, but people often do. I didn't think he was unwell.'

'You told the custody sergeant that you'd arrested my client on suspicion of theft and wished to keep him in custody in order to question him, is that right?'

'Yes, sir.'

'And my client said something to the sergeant?'

'Yes, sir. He said that he felt dizzy.'

'He felt dizzy,' I repeated. 'And what did

the custody sergeant do?'

'He placed him in a cell and phoned for the divisional surgeon.'

'And were you still present when the surgeon arrived?'

'Yes, sir. I was waiting with PC Allen to interview if the doctor passed him as fit.'

'Yes. Now, before he was placed in a cell, his property was taken from him, I believe?'

'Yes, sir.'

'Including two bottles of pills or capsules?'

'I think there was two, sir. It'll be on the Person In Custody form.'

'Yes, we'll come to that later, no doubt. Did my client say anything when the pills were taken from him?'

'Yes, sir. He said that they were his medication and that he needed them for his dizziness.'

'And what did the sergeant do?'

'He said that he might have them back if the doctor said it was all right.'

'So, he complains of feeling dizzy, his pills are taken from him and he is put in a cell to await the doctor. The doctor, we know, subsequently passed him as fit for interview and you and PC Allen conducted that interview, did you not?'

'Yes, sir.'

'Why was that interview not tape-recorded?

Surely it has been the practice of the Central Midlands force to tape interviews for a good many years now, or even to video them if they are complex. Why was this one not recorded?'

'I believe that it is perfectly within the law to make a written contemporaneous record of an interview, sir.'

'So it is, sergeant, and I was not seeking advice on the law. I was asking why this particular interview was conducted differently.'

'My recollection is that the station was very busy. The drugs squad had brought a number of people in from a raid and there was a queue for the two interview rooms.'

'So you decided to use the old procedure?'

'Yes, sir. Well, PC Allen suggested it and we asked Sergeant Grey if it was legal. He said it was and we took the accused to an office for the interview.'

'I see. Now, when you had finished that interview you charged him and bailed him, yes?'

'Yes, sir.'

'So he was not, in your opinion and that of the custody sergeant, a potential bail absconder?'

'No, sir.'

'Then, with all this queuing for interview rooms, and the fact that my client had complained of feeling dizzy, might it not have been better to have bailed him back to the station at a time when recording facilities would be available and interviewed him then?'

'With hindsight, sir, it might have been, but we had seen the girl and we wanted to finish the job if we could.'

'Ah, yes. You wanted a confession if you could possibly obtain one.'

'Mr Tyroll,' the Major interrupted. 'Are you suggesting that there was something improper in the procedure at the interview? The old process is still legal, is it not?' he added to his clerk.

'Certainly, Your Worship.'

'I am not suggesting,' I said, 'that the use of the old procedure was illegal. As to whether the interview was in any way improper, we have not got that far, but I am exploring the fact that the use of the written statement was unusual and that there was a reasonable alternative.'

'But not illegal,' remarked the Major.

'No, sir. Merely unusual,' I countered. He snorted.

'Mr Tyroll,' said the clerk, 'you have been pursuing your client's state of health at the time. Will you be calling medical evidence?'

This was my one piece of good luck. I had

extracted a report from Sawney's family doctor, who was most anxious not to appear in court. As a result I had cast his report in the form of what's called a 'Section Nine statement'. You send these to the other side and ask them to accept it in writing to avoid calling the witness. The Crown Prosecution Service showers defence lawyers with them, but when they get one served on them they go paranoid. They automatically assume that you're trying to slip something past them and they refuse to accept the written statement. Well, they usually do. This time they'd missed the deadline for objecting, so I had a right to use the written report.

'I shall not be calling a medical witness,' I said, smoothly. 'But, to avoid wasting the court's time, I have agreed a medical report with the Crown Prosecution Service and — '

The Prosecutor was on his feet, objecting as fast as an American. 'It is not the case, Your Worships, that we have agreed the Defence medical report. The fact is that a report was sent to our office in the Section Nine format and that, through an oversight, I admit, we failed to object within the limit.'

'What would you say to that, Mr Tyroll?' the clerk asked.

'Merely that the rules of this process are more than thirty years old, older indeed than the Crown Prosecution Service, and that they are incorporated in the text of the documents served, so that there need be no mistake. If the Prosecutor has failed to take the advantage which the law gives — whether through carelessness or any other reason — he must, I would argue, abide by the fruits of his carelessness.'

'Thank you, Mr Tyroll. Mr Patterson, I'm afraid I agree with Mr Tyroll and must advise Their Worships that the doctor's statement will be admissible.'

That was my second piece of luck.

I returned to the witness. 'So the surgeon having passed my client fit to be interviewed, you commenced an interview. I believe you asked the questions and PC Allen recorded the answers?'

'That's right, sir.'

'And, bearing in mind that, when first told the nature of your enquiries, my client had uttered a complete denial, was he at all reluctant to answer?'

'He wouldn't answer some questions at first, sir, but he became more co-operative.'

'And when PC Allen had written out his answers, he read it over, is that so?'

'Yes, sir.'

'And then he wrote this piece at the bottom — the caption — in his own writing?'

'Yes, sir. We have a card with the text on and he copied it out.'

'And then he signed the document?'

'Yes, sir.'

'Sergeant, was there any indication, during the entire interview, that my client was in any way unwell, or did not understand what was happening?'

'None at all, sir. It all happened as I have described.'

A witness who is able to completely deny something will do so. He will say, 'No.' When you get long answers you are probably dealing with a liar. For the first time I thought Sawney might be telling the truth.

'Would it surprise you, sergeant, to learn that my client says that he has almost no recollection of that interview, of making any statement, or of writing the caption, or signing the document?'

The officer eyed Sawney in the dock. 'I have no idea what the state of his mind or his memory may be at the present time, sir.'

PC Allen was no more helpful, merely echoing his partner's answers. Then we had the custody sergeant. He produced the Person In Custody form and explained how the two officers had presented Sawney at his desk and he had gone through the statutory procedure. When Sawney had complained of dizziness, the sergeant had called the divisional surgeon, who had examined Sawney and cleared him for interview. There being no interview room available, he had agreed with the arresting officers that they should fall back on the old procedure.

I examined the Person In Custody sheet before rising to cross-examine.

'Sergeant,' I began, 'was my client apparently well when he was first brought to you?'

'He was trembling, sir, but some people do when they've been arrested. I had no reason to suppose he was sick until he complained that he felt dizzy.'

'It says on the sheet that the arresting officers explained that they wished you to authorise the holding of my client in custody so that they could obtain evidence by questioning him. Right?'

'Yes, sir. That's the usual reason.'

'He then complained of dizziness and you called the surgeon?'

'Yes sir.'

'In the personal property listed on the form there are shown 'one small brown bottle of tablets' and 'one small white bottle of tablets'. Do you recall what tablets they were?'

He shook his head. 'No, sir. It was months ago and I have no recollection.'

'What did you do with them?'

'I put them in a property bag, zipped it up and locked it. He had them returned to him when he was bailed. His signature for them is on the form.'

'Did the surgeon see them?'

'Yes, sir. I drew his attention to them.'

'And the surgeon advised you that, in his opinion, my client was fit for interview?'

'Yes, sir. He told me that the suspect could be interviewed.'

'In fact, sergeant, that must have been your decision on the surgeon's advice. You are personally responsible at law for that decision, are you not?'

'Well, yes, sir.'

'When the interview ended, and my client was brought back to your desk to be charged and bailed, did you notice anything unusual about him then, sergeant?'

'It was a very busy time, sir. I had been concerned with his state before the interview because that was my duty, but I really don't remember anything about him afterwards.'

'So, sergeant, if he'd come out of the interview with his clothing torn, two black eyes and blood all over his face you wouldn't have noticed?'

'Mr Tyroll!' snapped the Major. 'What is the purpose of that question? Are you suggesting that your client was assaulted during the interview?'

'I am simply trying to determine, Your Worships, the extent of the sergeant's care for persons in custody. I have reminded him that he is personally responsible for suspects' fitness for interview. He is also personally responsible for the health and safety of detainees at all times while they are in custody.'

'He knows that,' said Billingham. 'Get on with it and try to stick to the point.'

The prosecutor closed his case with the custody sergeant and we adjourned for lunch.

27

Traditional lawyers' wisdom says that the Defence case never looks better than at the end of the Prosecution case. After that it's usually all downhill and that's without having Sawney as your only witness.

Police officers give evidence all the time. They learn how to do it. It's part of their professional expertise. Civilians are amateurs and they worry about appearing in the witness box. They think they're going to be made to look stupid and dishonest by smartass lawyers for the other side.

There are a few ground rules and if you stick to them a hostile advocate won't make much of you. First of all, keep your answers short. If you ramble on and try to explain things, you've far more chance of contradicting yourself or telling the cross-examiner something he didn't know. Secondly, if you can answer with 'Yes' or 'No', do so. If you can't, then there are only a few other safe answers. They are, 'I can't remember', 'I don't know' and 'I didn't hear/understand your question'. Finally keep your temper and don't argue.

Sawney knows all this, if only because I've reminded him every time I've represented him. He knows it, but he didn't do it.

He was uppity with me and kept trying to run on and explain things out of order and when I sat down the Prosecutor had a field day. Sawney dodged, argued, back-tracked, blethered on, snarled and fudged. Sometimes he didn't recall anything about the interview, sometimes he did; sometimes he had signed the statement, sometimes he couldn't remember. I just stared out of the window and wished I'd taken up digging ditches for a living.

It ended at last and I got my chance to put in the doctor's statement. I admit it sounded good. He said that he'd treated Sawney since childhood and that, in recent years, his patient had complained of increasing dizzy spells and fainting fits. He had prescribed medication for them (he didn't say when). He believed that Sawney suffered from a genetic condition which he called 'phenyl-cetonic'. It affects the chemistry of the blood and creates a predisposition to epilepsy, as well as causing prematurely grey hair. He believed that his patient might well have developed epilepsy and was having tests done. In his opinion, an epileptic suffered such severe disturbance of the brain during even a minor attack that he should not be asked to make any consequential decision or sign any document for as long as twenty-four hours afterwards.

Which was fine, as far as it went, but it only went as far as saying that Sawney might have this weird genetic condition, that he might have developed epilepsy as a result, and that — if he had — his statement was worthless. All very conditional. Still, it was all written in nice long words and it seemed to impress Their Worships.

Patterson, the Prosecutor, was still sulking about the medical evidence. He popped up and announced that he had the police surgeon outside and he would like the court's permission to call him in rebuttal of my medical report.

The clerk shook his head. 'Mr Patterson,' he reproved him, 'you know better than that. Had you taken the opportunity to object to Mr Tyroll's Section Nine statement, we should have had his doctor here for you to cross-examine him if you wished. You might also have called your own medical evidence. Indeed, forewarned as you were of the nature of the Defence evidence, I'm surprised that you didn't call the surgeon anyway. I shall have to advise Their Worships that it's too late now.'

Patterson sat down and sulked. We made

our closing remarks, me leaning heavily on the doctor's report. Their Worships retired for a smoke, a cup of tea, biscuits and to consider their verdict. Sawney sat in the dock and scowled at the police officers. I played hangman against myself on my notepad and lost.

The magistrates came back at last. Major Billingham leaned forward over the high bench and clasped his hands in front of him, clearing his throat.

'We have had some difficulties with this case,' he began. 'It seems to us that the defendant was quite properly arrested on suspicion and taken to be questioned. The custody sergeant acted entirely properly in calling in the divisional surgeon when the suspect made a complaint of dizziness and he could have done no other than accept the doctor's advice that the suspect was fit for interview. We place no blame upon the police doctor, who did not have the detailed knowledge of the defendant's own family doctor and cannot be expected to come across rare genetic disorders when he is called to a police station. With hindsight, it might have been better if Mr Tyroll's suggestion had been adopted and the defendant bailed to be interviewed on another occasion, but we appreciate the pressures upon our police to clear up detected crimes as fast as possible.'

Where this was going I was not sure, but it was the first time Billlingham had ever approved anything I had said and he was carefully letting everyone off the hook. I hoped that would include Sawney.

'We are entirely satisfied that what happened during the interview was exactly as the two officers have told us, but we cannot be sure of the defendant's perception of those events after hearing his doctor's report. Epilepsy is a dreadful affliction, and we sympathise deeply with those who suffer from it. Bearing in mind the doctor's strictures about the disturbance of the brain and the dangers of allowing a sufferer to take important decisions after even a minor episode, we cannot say that we are satisfied that his statement should be accepted as true and intentional. It is nobody's fault, but it is unfortunate that his medication was taken from him at the police station, though we understand the reasons why. Because of our unease about his perception of the interview, and for that reason only, we find the defendant Not Guilty.'

Not a word about the strange revival of the old interview format which meant we had no tape-recording. Nobody's fault, eh? Still, I'd won.

Sawney was out of the dock as fast as a rat, hissing in my ear, 'I want to sue them for wrongful arrest and false imprisonment!'

'You can't,' I said. 'The Bench has just said that everybody acted purely properly. Go home and say a very big thank you to your doctor.'

He scowled at me and left without another word.

In the lobby Patterson caught my arm and introduced me to the police doctor. 'He can tell you what those two bottles of pills were,' he said.

'Codeine and aspirin,' the doctor said. 'I jotted it down in my notes.'

I thanked him, grinned at Patterson and left. I don't know if Sawney was guilty. It's none of my business, anyway. I have to work with what he told me. Still — you wonder. When I first received the medical report I had a long search to find out about 'phenyl-cetonic' mutation. Apparently it causes eczema as well, which Sawney hasn't got, and the hair goes grey in childhood, which his didn't, but it may cause mental disturbance in adulthood, so maybe he has got it, and then there was that dodgy use of the old interview procedure. Maybe he really was innocent.

A day in court with Sawney, win or lose,

exhausts and depresses me, so I called briefly at my office, told them the result and caught a cab home.

Sheila couldn't understand my mood. 'You won, didn't you?' she said.

'Not really,' I said. 'I have a nasty suspicion that a cunning family doctor and an unscrupulous liar have just combined to get a petty thief out of his just deserts.'

'I thought you weren't supposed to worry about that,' she said.

'I'm not supposed to pre-judge my client, and I'm not an expert on genetic mutations, but I just can't escape the feeling that I have been used as a mouthpiece for a cynical scam, and I don't have to like it.'

'It must have happened before,' she said.

'Yes,' I agreed, 'and I've no doubt it will happen again, but I still don't have to like it. Pour me a large drink, please.'

Somehow the request made the doorbell ring and John Parry appear on the front doorstep. 'Make that two large drinks!' I called to Sheila.

'What about your clue?' Sheila demanded as she brought us our glasses. 'Any results?'

'That's what I called about,' John said. 'There were no prints on the tin, as we suspected, so we've opened it.'

He pulled an envelope from his pocket and

shook the contents on to the table, a number of capsules of two different types.

'Not more bloody pills!' I groaned. 'So, he takes stimulants for Dutch courage or sedatives to steady his nerves and he buys them illegally. Where does that get us?'

John shook his head. 'Not so,' he said. 'These are prescription jobs, so they may lead us to him. His little round tin was divided inside by a slip of cardboard and each half contained a clutch of different pills packed in cotton wool.'

'So what are they, then?' I asked.

He reached in his pocket for a slip of paper and read out, 'Nortriptyline and haloperidol.'

'I'm not the wiser,' I said.

'Well, the lab in Brum aren't doctors, but they say that nortriptyline is an anti-depressant.'

'What about the other?'

'I don't know yet. I've been trying to get hold of the police surgeon.'

'What about Macintyre?' I asked. 'He'll be at home. He doesn't have surgery or patients to call on.' Macintyre was the town's pathologist, an old crony of both me and John.

I rang Macintyre's number and found him at home.

'Mac,' I said, 'can you identify a couple of

drugs for John Parry and me?'

'What d'ye mean — identify?' he asked.

'I mean we know what they are, but we don't know what they do.'

'I'm not the best person to ask,' he said. 'I dinnae prescribe for my patients.'

'Come on, Doc. Some of your patients die of what's been prescribed for them and some of them take other things. You must know about the things people take.'

'Tell us what they are,' he demanded.

I read John's note to him. Macintyre muttered at the other end of the line. 'Nortriptyline', he said, 'is an anti-depressive drug, I believe. Give me a moment with the Pharmacopoeia. I'll look them up.'

He went away for a couple of minutes then returned with a sound of rustling pages.

'It says here', he said, 'that nortriptyline is an anti-depressant, as I thought, and haloperidol is an anti-psychotic.'

'What's that mean?'

'It means that it relieves symptoms caused by malfunctions of the brain. It can prevent or lessen physical spasms in some conditions.'

'What sort of conditions are we talking about, Doc?'

'How the hell do I know? Did ye get both of these from the same person?'

'Yes,' I said.

'Well, what sort of person is he? Is he epileptic or something?'

'We don't know, Doc. We've got the drugs but not their owner.'

'Then you're looking for someone who suffers from some kind of twitches and gets depressed about it. Tell that lassie of yours that I'm coming round for dinner tomorrow night to find all about what you're up to,' he said and put the phone down.

'Well,' I said, 'he wasn't in his most helpful mood, but he says that nortriptyline is an anti-depressant and that haloperidol is an anti-psychotic.'

'A what?' asked John.

'Apparently it offsets effects of brain malfunctions. He says it can prevent physical spasms.'

'What can cause physical spasms?' Sheila wondered.

'Doc only suggested maybe epilepsy.'

'Epilepsy,' said Sheila. 'Is that hereditary?'

'I believe that a predisposition for it can be inherited,' said John. 'You don't think I was right about a dynasty of brain surgeons with epilepsy?'

'There's a genetic mutation that can make epilepsy more likely,' I said, and told John briefly about Sawney and his possible phenyl-cetonic genes.

'Is it common?' he said.

I shook my head. 'The only figure I can find suggests less than fifty children a year born in the UK who have it.'

'That wouldn't be his motive, would it?' Sheila asked. 'Surely you wouldn't go to all that trouble to avoid people finding out there was epilepsy in the family, would you? I mean it's a terrible thing to have, but they can control it with modern drugs and anyway, if he told me that and asked me not to mention it, I wouldn't. It's not really relevant.'

'It wouldn't be just epilepsy,' I said. 'Our man's not just sick, he's crazy. He's unbalanced and fixated on something that needs to be hidden and he doesn't care much what he does to protect his secret.'

'What are you going to do, John?'

'First of all find a doctor who can tell me how rare this combination of drugs is and, hopefully, what you would take them for. Then circularise doctors looking for such a patient.'

'Doesn't sound quick,' I said.

'It won't be, I'm afraid, but it's the best we can do. We're already chasing the crossbow angle. That might produce something. By the way, he's writing to me now.'

'To you?'

'Yes, it seems he knows that I'm in charge

of this enquiry. I had this in the post today.'

He drew out a slip of white paper with a printed message:

WHO KILLED MCKENNA?
I, SAID THE SPARROW,
WITH MY LITTLE ARROW,
I KILLED MCKENNA.

'Does that mean he thinks he succeeded last night?' Sheila asked.

'Who knows? I think it's just another of his more or less relevant threats. I doubt if he'll try an arrow from the garden again. He'll expect us to be ready for that,' said John. 'But it does mean he's still trying — to stop you, if not to kill you.'

28

Sheila was extra attentive to me at breakfast next morning.

'What are you doing today?' she asked.

'I'm in court all morning,' I said. 'Why? What have you got on?'

'I thought I'd run up to Staffordshire and see Aunt Katy.'

The name didn't register for a moment, then, 'Ah! Your maiden lady who's descended from Jimmy Simmonds?'

'That's right.'

'I can't come with you,' I said. 'I really am stuck.'

'Don't let's have another blue about it, Chris. It's my problem and I've got to risk it.'

'It's my problem as well,' I said. 'And I don't like you going alone.'

'I know you don't and I'm grateful. But it's my fault he's after us, and you shouldn't be involved.'

'But I want to be involved. How do you think I'd feel if something happened to you and I wasn't there?'

'About as bad as you'd feel if you were there, I hope,' she said, with maddening logic.

'I'm going, Chris, and you've got your show to run.'

So I gave in, but I wasn't happy. I couldn't keep my mind off her all day and several times I had to pull myself up to avoid elementary errors in court. I was hugely relieved when I got home and found her already there. The smell of something exotic being cooked met me as I walked in.

'It's my turn in the galley,' I said.

'I'm taking Doc Macintyre at his word,' she said. 'He doesn't want to eat your cooking.'

'He's eaten it before. Anyway, Mac wants to eat anything that he hasn't had to cook himself. Tell me, why does Mac always warrant you cooking something special?'

'Because he's a nice old man who lives alone and drinks too much. I just want to give him a treat.'

'I'm a nice young man who lives alone and would drink too much if you'd let me.'

'You don't live alone. You have a beautiful and witty woman to share your bed, board and bath, not to mention cook your meals now and then.'

I changed tack. 'I take it, from your good mood, that Aunty Kate came up trumps, then?'

'Too right she did. You should hear about it!'

'I'm waiting.'

'Wait on. If I've got to tell Mac the whole rigmarole you can wait till then.'

Mac arrived with his customary bottle of Laphroaig. After a glass or two we sat down to one of Sheila's Pacific-rim specials and, over the food, she brought him up to speed on her researches and the backlash they'd provoked.

Dessert done she disappeared into the kitchen and returned, not with coffee, but with a bottle of champagne and glasses.

'We're celebrating?' I said. 'What are we celebrating?'

'That I'm a clever girl — that I've done it — that I've hit the bull's-eye — that I've solved the mystery!'

'You know who our nutter is?' I said.

'No!' she jeered 'Not that mystery! The real mystery!'

She popped and poured the champagne without another word of explanation, then produced her shoulder-bag and drew out a packet of photos. She laid one on the table. It was of a finger ring, apparently plain gold.

'That', she announced, 'is a ring which Kate Lewis inherited from her great-great-grandmother.'

'Who must have been Kate Evans, Jimmy Simmonds' sweetheart,' I said.

'Precisely, Watson. And this,' she said, laying down another photograph, 'is the inscription on the inside of that ring.'

The wording in the photograph said, 'My Kate — For Ever — J.S.'

Sheila laid her convict token down beside it 'That', she announced, 'is the ring that Jimmy Simmonds made and gave to his girl. That's his inscription inside it, and that is the writing and the work of the man who cut the token. Kate Lewis let me take her into Stafford to have the ring photographed and I took her to the Salt Library. I got her a copy of the song about Jimmy and we looked up his trial. He was done for stealing gold from his boss — he was a jeweller's apprentice — and the reason he was transported was probably because they never got the gold back and he wouldn't tell them where it went. My guess is that that's where it went,' and she pointed to the picture of the ring.

It didn't need an expert eye to see that she was right, about the inscription at least and maybe about the source of the gold ring. We toasted her.

'Congratulations,' I said. 'I never believed you'd actually find out who gave the token to who, but you made it.'

'Better yet,' she said, and put down another picture. It was a copy of a Victorian portrait of a middle-aged woman, with a small round face and large eyes. I guessed who it was. Now I could see the real face of the girl who slept on a Dorset beach.

'That,' Sheila confirmed, 'is Kate Evans, after she became Kate Lewis. This all puts the cherry on top of my book.'

'Doesn't it just!' I exclaimed. 'Mrs Wainwright will be disappointed, though.'

'So she will, but Kate Lewis was delighted. That ring has come down through the women of her family and was always said to have belonged to Kate Evans, but they could never understand the inscription because they knew her husband was called Thomas Lewis.'

We took another round of champagne for the picture, then Mac said, 'All ye've got to do now is stop your loony, lassie,' which brought us back to reality.

'Mac,' I said, 'have you had any further thoughts on what sort of illness our man might have?'

He shook his head. 'There's a whole heap of peculiar conditions of the brain that it might be, and any one of them would make you depressed. I was thinking last night if I'd ever dealt with someone who'd been taking those two drugs, but I canna recall a case.'

If Mac couldn't recall it, he hadn't had it. 'Do you think his disease might be the thing that's driving him on?' I asked.

'It may well be what makes him crazy enough to do what he's doing,' he said, 'but I can't see that he would be that anxious to keep it a secret.'

'John Parry suggested a family of brain surgeons who've gone bonkers,' Sheila said.

'He would,' Mac grunted. 'If policemen had less overheated imaginations we wouldna have to have a Court of Appeal. I suppose if you were a wealthy surgeon or a top-class airline pilot or the President of the United States, you wouldnae want people knowing you'd got some kind of brain-rot that sent you doolally and made you twitch. Have you got any such among the people you've ferreted out, Sheila?'

'I don't think so,' she said, but she went and fetched her files.

Soon we were all poring over a table full of family trees, looking for any signs of hereditary madness.

Mac pointed to the Lewis/Jones chart. 'There's two there that ended up in a funny farm. What about them? Do you know any more?'

'Kate Lewis says they were harmless. They just exposed themselves and talked nonsense, so they got locked up. She says one of her distant cousins is the same. He's in

Burntwood Hospital now.'

'That's not necessarily reliable evidence,' I said. 'That family hid the fact that Kate Evans' son was illegitimate and that his father had been transported.'

'Maybe,' said Sheila, 'but I'm sure she told me the truth about the recent one. She knew him, used to play with him as a kid. She says he's harmless.'

Mac was peering at the Bradleys. 'There's a bit of peculiarity here,' he said. 'His granny went funny in her old age and his dad died young.'

'Yes, but from pneumonia,' Sheila said.

'Pneumonia kills little kiddies and old folks. It only kills hale adults if they're damned careless.'

'But he hasn't gone funny — Ian Bradley. He's only got arthritis,' protested Sheila.

'If you had it, you wouldnae say 'only',' said Mac. 'Still, you're right. There's no pattern of illness or death there.'

We peered a lot and argued a lot and drank a lot, but even with Mac's help we couldn't evolve any useful information from Sheila's charts.

Mac called a cab and departed eventually. We washed up and Sheila turned in. I made my nightly security round. In the sitting-room the smashed window had been replaced, but we had not used the room since the attack. Somehow it seemed too vulnerable, though the kitchen windows faced the garden as well. I ambled round, checked the locks on the repaired window and noted how well Mrs Dunk had cleared up the glazier's messy traces. The record that Sheila had been about to play was where Mrs Dunk had put it, on top of the player, so I slid it back into the right shelf.

We fell asleep quickly, probably because of the amount of champagne, wine and whisky we'd put down. I woke up about an hour later, from a nightmare. I saw myself as a little boy, back with my mother at the Brooklyn Hospital where she and I had called on Woody Guthrie. We had sat on a sunlit balcony, above tree-tops, and this nice little smiling man had sung me some of his famous children's songs. In my dream he wasn't smiling, he was scowling, and he wasn't singing funny songs, he was leaning forward, counting my toes, which for some reason were bare, and singing:

> 'This little piggy was nosy,
> This little piggy wouldn't stop,
> This piggy wouldn't be warned,
> This little piggy got the chop.'

299

All the time he was singing I was terrified of what would happen when it ended. It ended when he shouted the word 'Chop' at me and leapt across the space towards me. I woke up sweating.

As I lit a cigarette I wondered about the dream. With the door to my subconscious still half-open from dreaming, images and phrases began to pop into my memory. I took the pad that I keep beside the phone and started to scribble. I filled several pages and went back and forwards over them.

It still didn't quite make sense, but I had a strong feeling that there was a pattern in my scribbles. After two more cigarettes I slid quietly out of bed and padded down to the library. In criminal law you never know what you're going to need to look up, so my shelves were crammed with all sorts of reference books. I knew the facts I needed were there somewhere.

It took half an hour to find it and another hour to make it slot into the gaps in my scribbles, but in the end I had it. The only bit I still didn't understand was about the spiders.

Sheila woke up as I clambered back into bed. 'Where have you been? What's the matter?' she asked. 'Why can't you sleep?'

I told her about my nightmare.

'I thought you said you liked him, that he sang funny songs to you.'

'I did, and he did. But I know now what it was. I've got it.'

'What? Indigestion?'

'No — the answer! I know who it is and why it is. I know how he's doing it and why he's doing it! What's more, I think I know how to catch him.'

'Well, tell then.'

'It's too late,' I said. 'And I'm tired and still half-drunk. I'll tell you in the morning. You'll have to write him a letter.'

'Ratbag!' she said.

29

I woke to find Sheila sitting on the side of the bed studying my notepad.

'I don't understand this,' she said when she saw that I was awake.

I struggled to get a grip on what had blossomed from slippery suggestions to absolute certainties the night before, and started to explain my jottings.

'And this was because you had a dream?' she said at one point.

'Martin Luther King had a dream,' I said.

'Yair,' she said, 'and they shot him.'

'Dreams', I said, 'are the way your subconscious tells you what you've forgotten you know.'

'Just suppose you're right,' she said. 'What happens next? Did you say I should write to him? What does he do then — write back saying, 'Dear Dr McKenna, I'm frightfully sorry', and then flush himself down the dunny?'

I took the pad and scribbled a draft of a letter. She looked at it suspiciously.

' 'I have been reviewing my computer files after our interview and find that there are aspects of your family's history, especially the question of your son, which seem to require clarification',' she read. 'Why don't I just ask him for another meeting?'

'That's the whole point,' I said. 'I don't like you being a target. This way he'll think you know what he's hiding and that you've got the info on your computer.'

'So what?'

'So, he'll come after the computer. Then we can nail him — redhanded. Make John's case for him.'

'A bit less of the red,' she said, but she wrote the letter before I left the house.

I had no intention of telling John Parry about my ideas until I had set the game in motion. After that he could join in or not.

As soon as I reached my office I called in Alasdair and Jayne, my long-serving secretary, and outlined the situation to them. Alasdair was critical at first, but gradually came round to my way of thinking. That was a big plus. Jayne didn't pretend to follow the argument but was prepared to give it a go and loves dressing up anyway.

Detective Inspector Parry was a tougher nut to crack. He heard me out over a sandwich lunch in my office, with an almost immovable expression of disbelief.

'And this started with a dream?' he said,

when I'd finished.

'Freud and Jung were both pretty excited by dreams,' I said.

'Neither of them,' he said, 'were detectives, as I recall. There's no way of checking any of this, is there?'

'You might try Interpol,' I suggested.

He nodded. 'And if they've never heard of him?'

'It doesn't invalidate my argument, does it? If they have, then it may be a little support.'

He picked at the crumbs in his sandwich paper. 'I don't like it,' he said. 'It's dangerous.'

'If I'm wrong,' I said, patiently, 'then there's no harm done. If I'm right, he'll wait till the first time he knows Sheila and I are out, then he'll go for her computer. If he thinks that the secret he's trying to hide is on her machine, he won't dare attack her until he's destroyed the machine.'

He was silent for a long time. Then, 'If you're right — and I'm not saying you are — why don't I search his two addresses?'

'Because, for all we know, he's got a third — or a fourth, or a fifth. Where'll we be if we tip him off and don't catch him? The beauty of my way is that he'll have to make a try. It's back to tethering a goat under a tree to draw him out of the jungle, only this time the goat isn't Sheila. She can stay well away from it.'

'Fat chance!' he snorted. 'Keeping that girl away from a fight would take rhinoceroses. And you expect me to go along with this — officially?'

'I don't care whether you go along with it officially or not. I'd prefer you to go along with it, though.'

'But if I don't — you'll do it anyway, won't you?'

'Think of another way,' I challenged.

He heaved a long sigh. 'All right, boyo,' he said at last. 'I must be almost as daft as you. But it will be unofficial. I can't go around entrapping people. I'd have all the lefty lawyers in Britain on my back. You get our man bang to rights and I will charge him, but the charge will arise out of the success of routine police precautions, won't it?'

'Oh, absolutely,' I agreed.

He was right about the rhinoceroses. I gave Sheila's letter time to reach the suspect before setting the trap. When I finally explained the set-up to her she asked, 'Where do I fit into all this?'

'You don't,' I said. 'That's the good part. You can stay well clear.'

'No way!' she said. 'You forget, I have got some serious defongerating of this ratbag to do.'

'I'm trying to set him up for John and his boys.'

'Good!' she said. 'They can have what's left!'

'I'll arrange so you can be close at hand when he's nicked,' I said.

'That's right,' she said. 'You'll arrange it so that I'm right there.'

We began with the equipment arriving in the afternoon, in the same van that brought Alasdair and Jayne up the back lane to the back garden gate. While Alasdair and I set up the gear, Jayne and Sheila prowled through Sheila's wardrobe.

At last we had everything in place — an infra-red video camera mounted inside the sitting-room window, feeding a video-recorder and a small black and white monitor. We stood a large draught excluder behind the monitor and drew the curtains, so that the screen's glow would not be visible from outside after dark, then Alasdair went upstairs and shaved off his moustache.

I had left the kitchen door open and one by one John arrived, followed by a detective sergeant and a constable. 'There will be a couple of plain-clothes lads front and back once it's dark,' John said. 'We're only here because Interpol says you guessed right — convictions for theft and arson in West

Germany and the Netherlands in the 1960s. Maybe you're right about the rest.'

'I don't want him frightened off,' I said.

'Never fear, bach. They're highly trained officers who can melt into the landscape. He won't spot them. Have you laid on refreshments?'

'After dark,' I said. 'Meanwhile, take your blokes in the sitting-room and see if you approve the set-up.'

Jayne and Alasdair came downstairs, Alasdair moustacheless with his hair ruffled to resemble as nearly as possible my thick curls, Jayne in Sheila's safari suit and an ash-blonde wig. Sheila had even loaned her hefty leather shoulder-bag to aid the deception.

'Do you think we'll pass?' Jayne said, pirouetting in the hall.

'He's only going to get a glimpse of you getting into the car and maybe passing by in the car. He'll swallow it,' I said.

'And all we have to do is drive away?' Alasdair checked.

'Right, and stay away until I ring you on the mobile. We can't have you arriving back at the wrong moment.'

'What if you haven't rung by the time the pubs shut?' Alasdair asked.

'I don't know! Go to a night-club or

something! Just stay away until you get the all-clear from me!'

'And this is all on expenses?' Jayne said. 'Al, switch the mobile off and we'll stay out all night!'

'No chance!' I said. 'He'll be here as soon as it's well dark.'

'Just make sure Sheila's all right,' commanded Jayne, 'and you, of course.'

We switched off all lights in the house and Jayne and Alasdair made their exit into Sheila's car and away.

'Right!' I said to the assembled company in the sitting-room. 'From now on, nobody switches a light on, nobody goes near a window, nobody makes a loud noise, and anyone who wants a smoke goes into the passage before lighting up. Any other orders, John?'

He shook his head. 'No,' he said, 'that's about it, except for warning the civilians present that, if our man shows up, he'll certainly be armed in some way, so stay out of the way while we sort him.'

Sheila brought in trays of sandwiches and jugs of soft drinks We settled down to wait, each taking a thirty-minute turn at watching the monitor for signs of activity.

The early evening movement of cars and people in the street died away and everything became very still. An occasional car went through the street but otherwise all we heard were the distant sounds of the town down the hill. On the monitor screen nothing moved. John's two point men reported by radio that they were in place, one watching the side gully and one watching the back lane.

As it grew dark the quiet conversation in the sitting-room lapsed into silence. Now we were all watching the little monitor with its unnaturally bright image of the lawn and the shrubs.

A dog began to bark somewhere outside. 'He's on his way,' I said.

John's radio crackled and a voice said softly, 'Fido One here. Target entering alley.'

'Roger. Stay put,' John responded.

It seemed like ages before the radio came to life again. 'Fido Two,' said a voice, 'target at rear gate.'

'Roger. Stay put,' John commanded, and we all leaned closer to the monitor screen.

In the far right-hand corner of the picture the gate moved slowly, swinging cautiously open, and a blurred figure slipped in and slid behind the shrubs alongside the gate.

'We've got him!' I breathed, finally satisfied that I had been right.

Time passed and nothing more moved.

'What's he up to?' whispered John's sergeant.

'He's making sure that the house is really empty,' I said. 'Have you got your mobile phone, John? Ring my number and let it ring for ages. That ought to convince him.'

John took out his phone and keyed my number. The phones in the sitting-room and the study sprang to life, yelping in harmony.

'He ought to be able to hear them from where he is,' I said.

John cut the phones off. We waited again. After a few seconds the shrubs stirred. A face looked out, then a figure stepped on to the lawn.

'That's the lodger from up the street!' exclaimed John's detective constable. 'I interviewed him the other night.'

'That's right,' I said. 'Watch!'

He was walking steadily but cautiously across the lawn, both hands held in front of him. As he drew closer to the camera I saw that he was carrying something in both hands. Suddenly I saw the gap in my clever plan. He wasn't going to burgle us.

I slipped out into the kitchen, where the door was still unlocked, and took a cautious look through the window. Our man was still steadily advancing on the house.

'Leave him to me!' John's voice hissed in my ear.

'He's carrying another bomb!' I said. 'I've got to tackle him before he gets close enough to throw it.'

'Leave it to a rugby player!' he commanded.

'I am one,' I said.

'Public school stuff,' he sneered.

I didn't wait to argue. I slid out of the door and pounded across the lawn. As he heard me coming the intruder swivelled, saw me, and raised his hand to throw. I silently thanked God for a headmaster who believed that soccer was a low game played by hooligans and took my target below the knees.

He crumpled, but the bomb flew from his hand. I forced him into the ground and cowered over him, waiting for the explosion. Behind me, John Parry leapt like a dancer to catch the device and in one continuous movement flung it into the pond.

My captive was heaving and cursing beneath me. With John's help I stood up and we pulled him to his feet. I knocked off his hat, pulled off his glasses and pulled away the thick false moustache.

'Ian Bradley,' said John, 'I am arresting you on suspicion of attempted murder, criminal damage, sending dangerous devices through the Royal Mail, sending anonymous threats, theft of a briefcase, theft of a motor car, cruelty to a cat, and probably several other things that I haven't thought of yet. You do not have to say anything, but if you do not mention anything which you later rely on in your defence it may be to your disadvantage.'

The other officers had joined us and we took Bradley back into the sitting-room. As the sergeant switched on the light, Bradley slumped into a chair, wheezing and twitching. I thought about Mrs Dunk's neighbour's lodger, who'd been apparently drunk and twitching immediately after the arrow was fired — when his disease hit him and he hadn't got his medication because he'd dropped his pills in my garden. Bradley groped inside his coat and the sergeant grabbed his hand, forcing it open to reveal another tin, like the one he had dropped before.

John screwed it open and examined the pills inside. 'Looks the same,' he said. 'How many of which, Mr Bradley?'

'One of each,' Bradley gasped. Sheila was beside him in a flash with a glass of water helping him take the capsules and sip the water.

He heaved and shuddered for a few

minutes, then became stiller.

'I suppose I should apologise, Dr McKenna,' he said.

'You might at that,' she said.

'I had to do it. I had to try and stop you finding out.'

'I wasn't looking for that,' she said. 'I wouldn't have found it and anyway I'd never have used it.'

He shook his head from side to side. 'I couldn't risk it. I couldn't risk it,' he said. 'I thought you were bound to find out. When you wrote to me I thought you must have found out from the pills I dropped.'

'I only found out,' I said, 'because, as a child, I met a man called Woody Guthrie.'

His head jerked up. 'Guthrie?' he said. 'You knew Guthrie? Then you know what happened to him?'

'That's right,' I said. 'I know that he became sick of a strange disease that doctors thought was drunkenness, that it took years for it to be correctly diagnosed and that then it turned out to be Huntington's chorea — a hereditary disease that attacks the brain and invariably kills. It took me a long time — rather too long — but I finally put the pieces together. I remembered Guthrie and I remembered a man who pretended to have arthritic hands; I remembered a music teacher who pretended he hadn't got a wife and son and who told us that he'd found one child who was a prodigy; I recalled a man whose wife thought he drank when he didn't, who had bursts of temper for no reason so that she left him; and a man whose postman saw him dancing in the garden — not dancing, really, was it? It was the spasms from the disease, wasn't it? I remembered that your grandmother came from Venezuela, where fifteen thousand or so people from one family carry the gene that causes Huntington's; I remembered that your father died of pneumonia, which kills the lucky Huntington's victims, I recalled a car with two cans of soft drinks to quench the unnatural thirst that victims have, and I knew what had happened.'

I lit a cigarette. 'You went to the Family Centre to track your ancestry and see where the disease came from. You discovered your transported ancestor, but that didn't matter, you'd also caught on that it was your South American grandmother who brought the faulty gene into the family. It didn't matter until you accidentally discovered that someone who was writing a book was researching your family. Then you panicked.'

'I couldn't help it,' he whispered. 'I had to stop it. You could have ruined my son.'

314

'Has he got the gene?' I asked. 'Has he been tested?'

'No, no, of course not. He must never, ever know. It would destroy him.'

'Then he might not have it. But you weren't willing to take the chance. You tracked Sheila, tapped her computer from one of the websites, stole her briefcase and her car, broke into my garden, slaughtered our poor bloody cat. I should have caught on. A man who watched us all the time — who knew when we were in or out — an old man who walked his dog along here all the time — a respectable lodger doing research — a man who had read Stevenson as a boy and used the name 'Mr Hyde' for his other personality. You could see this house from your bedroom window up the road, couldn't you? I should have realised that a man who read *The Lore and Language of Schoolchildren* might be amused by children's rhymes and that a science teacher might know how to make a reasonable bomb or two. I should have remembered a dog-kennel with no dog and a dog that barked just before you fired your crossbow. I should have known it all far sooner.'

I was running off at the mouth because I was angry — angry at this sad little man who huddled in an armchair and angry at myself for not putting the pieces together sooner, for leaving Sheila at risk.

'Well, you know it all now,' he said. 'And soon everybody will know and my boy will be destroyed.'

'There's no need for anyone to know,' I said, 'and you've forgotten something about Woodrow Wilson Guthrie.'

'What's that?' he said.

'The disease killed him when he was little older than you, but before then he'd written hundreds of songs, become world-famous and inspired people like Bob Dylan and Phil Ochs and Tom Paxton and Billy Bragg. Even if your boy has it, he can still make the grade.'

'But if people know, nobody will train him, nobody will take him seriously!'

'Will there be a trial?' Sheila asked John.

'I doubt it. He's evidently a very sick man.'

'I have been keeping alive on chemicals and my hopes for my boy,' Bradley said.

John picked up his radio. 'Fido One, Fido Two,' he said. 'Collect the dog from the gully and bring the cars to the front. We're going back to the nick.'

Bradley hauled himself to his feet. 'I am sorry, Dr McKenna. I didn't want to harm you — really.'

'Yair,' she said. 'Maybe not. Your son may

316

be in my book, Mr Bradley, but your family secret won't — fair dos?'

He nodded. As the officers gathered around him to take him out, I stopped them for a moment.

'There's one thing I don't know,' I said. 'What about the spider? Was that just a lucky guess?'

He looked ashamed. 'That was wrong,' he said. 'When I took the briefcase there was a magazine in there. It had one of those silly personal questionnaires in it with a question about 'What is your darkest secret?' Dr McKenna had written that she hated spiders.'

'You keep my secrets and I'll keep yours,' she said as they led him out.

We stood at the door with our arms around each other's waists as they loaded Bradley into a police car.

'What about all this defongerating you were going to do?' I asked.

'Poor bastard,' she said. 'He's been well and truly defongerated by life. Do you reckon his kid has got it?

'I don't know,' I said. 'It's fifty-fifty. Toss of a penny stuff.'

We do hope that you have enjoyed reading this large print book.

Did you know that all of our titles are available for purchase?

We publish a wide range of high quality large print books including:
Romances, Mysteries, Classics
General Fiction
Non Fiction and Westerns

Special interest titles available in large print are:
The Little Oxford Dictionary
Music Book
Song Book
Hymn Book
Service Book

Also available from us courtesy of Oxford University Press:
Young Readers' Dictionary
(large print edition)
Young Readers' Thesaurus
(large print edition)

For further information or a free brochure, please contact us at:
Ulverscroft Large Print Books Ltd.,
The Green, Bradgate Road, Anstey,
Leicester, LE7 7FU, England.
Tel: (00 44) 0116 236 4325
Fax: (00 44) 0116 234 0205

Antique dealing has its own equivalent to 'insider trading', as Charles Ramsay finds out to his cost. Offered the purchase of a lifetime, he sees all his ambitions realised in an antique jade cup, known as the 'Loot'. But as soon as the deal is irrevocably struck he finds himself stuck with it like an albatross around his neck — unable to export it without a licence, unable to sell it at home, and in a paralysing no man's land where nobody has sufficient capital to take it off his hands . . .

NO TIME LIKE THE PRESENT

June Barraclough

Daphne Berridge, who has never married, has retired to the small Yorkshire village of Heckcliff where she grew up, intending to write the biography of an eighteenth-century woman poet. Two younger women are interested in her project: Cressida, Daphne's niece, who lives in London, and is uncertain about the direction of her life; and Judith, who keeps a shop in Heckcliff, and is a divorcee. When an old friend of Daphne falls in love with Judith, the question — as for Cressida — is marriage or independence. Then Daphne also receives a surprise proposal.